2023

COME
HOME
SAFE

BRIAN BUCKMIRE

COME HOME SAFE

A Novel

BLINK®

BLINK

Come Home Safe
Copyright © 2023 by Brian G. Buckmire

Requests for information should be addressed to:
Blink, *3900 Sparks Dr. SE, Grand Rapids, Michigan 49546*

ISBN 978-0-310-14218-8 (hardcover)
ISBN 978-0-310-14223-2 (audio download)
ISBN 978-0-310-14222-5 (ebook)

Cover Design: Micah Kandros
Interior Design: Denise Froehlich

Printed in the United States of America

23 24 25 26 27 / LSC / 10 9 8 7 6 5 4 3 2 1

IN MEMORY OF OLIVE REID

May these words help keep children safe, as your words continue to keep your children safe, and their children, and theirs.

PART 1

COME HOME SAFE:

From the Subway

CHAPTER 1

It's Easier to Build Than Repair

Frederick Douglass

"*FOURTEEN, FIFTEEN, SIXTEEN* . . ." Reed counts out loud as he juggles his soccer ball from his knee to his head in the park. He's always carried a soccer ball wherever he goes, but lately it's been an almost constant presence. And the stakes of today's practice are high because he's determined to play for the Elijah McCoy High School varsity team. After he put his name on the tryout sheet, the coach smiled at him and said, "You know if you make the team, you'll be the first freshman to make varsity? But no pressure, right?" Reed knows he has to be more than good enough to make the team because of that fact, so every little bit of practice counts—even if it's just a few minutes of fooling around in the park across the street from Public Middle School 416 while he waits to pick up his little sister.

Last year, Reed could just meet Olive at her locker after school, and their parents would drive them both home. But this year is different. Their parents still drop them off at Olive's school in the morning, but it's Reed's responsibility to get Olive and himself home safe at the end of the day. He'd already done the easy part—walking the couple blocks from Elijah McCoy High School to Olive's school—and now they simply had to take the train home together.

"Getting your sister home from school each day is a big responsibility, but your mother and I trust you," Reed's dad had told him when he dropped them off at the beginning of the week. Reed felt proud that they trusted him to watch his little sister now. Even though Olive got on his nerves sometimes.

Reed notices Olive walk out the front door of the school and wave goodbye to her friends. As she stands at the top of the stairs, she looks across the street at Reed and pantomimes juggling a soccer ball. He knows Olive thinks he is obsessed with soccer. But so is their dad, so it's no surprise where Reed gets it from. Reed started playing soccer when he was three and fell in love with it. Now, he plays all over the city with his travel team, even going to overnight tournaments in different states. His dad, who played soccer himself growing up, sometimes played with Reed in the morning before they got ready for the day.

Reed continues to count as he juggles the ball. "Twenty-six, twenty-seven, twenty-eight—"

"Boo!" a raspy voice calls from behind him.

Startled, Reed drops the ball. "Ugh! I almost got to thirty!" Reed looks to the sky as if to ask, *Why?*

Olive flashes a fake innocent smile. "You're easy to spot from a distance, I'll give you that."

"Why's that? Because of my soccer ball?" Reed asks.

"Yeah, and because of your outfit. If you weren't so baby-faced, you'd look like you work at some hipster corporate job in Red Hook."

If Reed loves anything more than soccer, it's looking good, which means he's always well dressed when he leaves the house. Today he's wearing his brand-new white high-tops with gold studs, a pink button-up dress shirt, and an old blue-and-brown blazer with brown suede elbow patches that Dad got him for his birthday after he begged for one just like his. Reed had even stuffed a little pocket square in the jacket, just to add some "flare."

Reed has to admit that Olive looks good too, for the most part. Her school uniform still looks neatly pressed as always, and her hair is braided then let out at the ends, with a pencil sticking out from behind her ear. The pencil is an Olive staple, half chewed and dull, constantly looking like it's on its last leg.

"Ready to go, bro?" Olive asks.

"Yeah, I'm ready," he says, walking over to his ball. Reed picks up his backpack and slings it over his shoulders, kicks the ball into the air, catches it, and then tucks it under his arm as they walk toward the subway stop.

"Hey! How was debate team practice?" Reed asks, pointing at the little notebook in Olive's hand.

"Pretty good," she says, shuffling through her old, beat-up, and dog-eared notebook. Reed looks down at her notebook to see it's full of the random notes she jots down whenever she gets a new idea or sees something she doesn't want to forget.

"We just picked little things to debate. Burgers versus hot dogs. Fall versus spring. You know, things we don't have to research. Next week, we're going to start learning the rules for debate competitions. Our first competition is coming up in a month. It's pretty cool getting to argue different topics in class. Reminds me of when Dad is in the middle of a trial."

"It's no soccer," Reed says with a laugh, "but it's pretty cool, I guess. Still a competition. Plus, I would never want to argue with you."

"Debate, not argue. And I'll take that as a compliment, thank you very much." She grins. "Hey, wasn't today the day you could sign up for the varsity tryouts?"

"Yeah!" Reed says. "The coach gave me a permission slip to take home because I'm the only freshman to try out for the team this year, and he wants to make sure Mom and Dad are okay with it. And get this," Reed adds confidently, "a freshman has never made the varsity team—ever. But I'm going to be the first—watch, you'll see." Reed stares at his soccer ball, eyes filled with hope. "This is going to be a great year."

"Even I wouldn't debate that," Olive says with a smile.

"Corny, but good one." Reed laughs.

Reed and Olive reach the Utica Avenue subway station. As they approach the stairs leading down to the subway platform, they pass three boys, all a little older than Reed, hanging out at the entrance.

"Hey, is that the kid who plays center defense for the Brooklyn Energy? Reed! What's good?" one of the boys yells.

"The Great Wall of Brooklyn!" another boy shouts as he walks toward Reed with a goofy smile on his face, arms open wide open in welcome.

"Hey guys, 'sup?" Reed says and fist-bumps the boys one by one, feeling a little thrill at being recognized.

"You know, just hanging out after school before practice tonight," one of the boys says. "Yo, we saw you guys at the Labor Day Tournament. Congrats on the win! Respect. We watched you score that header in the finals. *Golaso!*" He clicks his fingers.

It feels good to be complimented on his skills. And this isn't the first time this group has given him praise.

Reed doesn't really know them by name, because he's only bumped into them at tournaments before. They're at least three years older, but they've always congratulated him after big games, starting when he was new to middle school. Some of them even said he was good enough to play with them.

"What's with the ball? You going to practice soon too?" another boy asks.

"Naw, tryouts for my high school team are starting up tomorrow. I'm just trying to get in some extra touches, you know? Get this: my school has never had a freshman on the varsity team before. I'mma be the first after this year though," Reed proclaims with a smile.

One of the boys laughs as he daps Reed. "Respect, King! You definitely got this. High school soccer is weak anyway—we've been beating teams without trying. And bro, you don't need extra touches—you good. We've seen you play. You're like the best center back your age. The varsity coach is a fool if he doesn't scoop you up."

Two of the other boys turn to each other and they laugh. One of them says, "Hey, remember that time you were on a breakaway and Reed caught up to you and slide tackled the ball from you?" He elbows his friend.

"Naw, I don't remember that," the boy says as he looks to the sky. The two laugh again.

"Hey, come hang out with us, Reed. You don't need to practice. If anything, you need a little something to relax, and we got just the thing for you," one says as he pulls a squished joint out of his pocket.

Reed laughs awkwardly. "Naw, guys, I'm good. I'm not really into that stuff. Plus, I gotta drop my sister off."

The boy lights the joint and waves it in front of Reed. "C'mon, mon," he says, imitating a Jamaican accent. "I thought you were Jamaican. You don't want a little ganja, mon?" The boy laughs, takes a hit of the joint, and then coughs.

"C'mon, it's not like it's illegal or anything," someone else in the group says. "No one cares anymore in NYC; it's just weed. What are they going to do, give you a warning?"

"Isn't his pops some kind of public defender too? Why is he so worried?" the third boy says, nudging the others.

They're right. Reed's dad started working as a public defender in the Brooklyn office way before Reed and Olive were born. He taught Olive everything she knows about the law. Now, their family jokes that one day she'll be a judge, but she always corrects them and says she's going to be a justice on the Supreme Court. Reed isn't as interested in the law, but his dad still taught him how to be safe when speaking with police officers, how to de-escalate interactions with them, and how to invoke his rights. "Knowledge is power, and preparation keeps you safe," Reed's dad always reminds him.

"You're right, it really isn't a crime in New York any-more, at least if you're over twenty-one, and it probably should have never been a crime. But that's not the point." Olive's little voice breaks through the teenage boys' cackling. They look around with confused expressions, clearly having forgotten Olive has been there the whole time. "Sure, weed is legal in New York. But only in small amounts. Like, if you have over three ounces of it, that's a crime, and it's definitely illegal for kids to have. And cops can still stop you, detain you, and maybe even search you if they see you smoking or even smell it on you. But my real point is, we're about to take the train and don't need that headache. So we're out, boys." Having made her announcement, Olive walks confidently past the boys and down the stairs to the subway station.

The three boys stand there, frozen.

Reed chuckles, breaking the silence. "What she said." He nods toward Olive. "I'll see you guys around," he says as he catches up to Olive at the bottom of the stairs. Olive walks up to the turnstile waiting for Reed, MetroCard in hand. She swipes her card and walks through. Reed follows behind her.

A sign overhead says, "Next train to Manhattan: 2 mins away."

Above the sign on the wall is a big ad with a piece of plastic in front of it. It must be brand-new because it shines like a mirror. Reed stands in front of it, checking himself out and fixing his clothes, making sure his shirt is straight, his jacket is fitting right, and his shoes are clean.

The station speakers chime and a scratchy voice from a platform speaker announces, "Next train to Manhattan will arrive in one minute."

"You done prettying yourself up? Train's about to pull in," Olive says.

Reed rolls his eyes. "You're going to need a new joke, Olive," he says, giving one last look at the "mirror" and fixing his jacket collar.

"Hey!" Reed hears a shout from behind him. "Hey! Stop!"

"Cops! Go! Go! Go!" The shouts tumble down the stairs where Olive and Reed were just moments ago. As the train comes speeding into the station, the siblings hear short screams in between the train's screeches. The voices sound far away because the train is making so much noise.

"Stop! Don't move!"

"Hurry down the stairs."

"Go! Go! Go!"

Reed can only make out some of the voices. A few sound like the boys they saw at the top of the stairs, but the other voices don't sound familiar. Reed and Olive both turn.

Far from Reed and Olive, the three boys from earlier come sprinting down the stairs, laughing and cackling. One boy is still clutching a squished joint between his fingers. He takes one last pull before throwing it aside. The boys barrel through the turnstiles, two hurdling over them like Olympic athletes, one sliding underneath.

Reed and Olive exchange looks as they watch the figures run down the other end of the platform. The siblings walk down the platform, away from the shouting, to where the front of the train will be. The boys head toward another set of stairs that lead back up to the street, but Reed doesn't look to see where they go. *It's none of our business*, he thinks. "Let's keep walking up the platform a little more," he says to Olive as the lights of the train come shining through the tunnel and into the station.

The train screeches to a halt as it pulls into the station. The doors swing open.

They duck onto the train as the yelling echoes in the distance, down the subway platform. "Just another day in Brooklyn," Olive says to Reed.

There are two open seats near the middle of the car; the siblings sit in one of the pair of seats that is perpendicular to the train car. Olive sits down first, closest to the window, and Reed settles next to her, legs facing outward so he has more space to stretch out. Olive tugs at Reed's jacket and then practically leaps into a seat. Reed slowly walks over and takes the seat next to her. It won't take many stops for them to get home, but they have some time to kill. Reed reaches into his jacket pocket and pulls out his headphones. He puts them in his ears just as his phone blasts, "Goooalll!" Quickly, he turns the volume down. He never turns the sound on his phone up all the way when he's out of the house. Reed's dad always tells him to be aware of his surroundings, to make sure he has use of all of his senses at all times, especially when he's alone with his sister. After adjusting his headphones for comfort, Reed turns in his seat, leans back, and puts his foot up on the edge of the empty seat in front of him, just in case someone wants to sit. Then he scrolls to the next soccer highlight video.

"Next stop, Franklin Avenue, Medgar Evers College," a voice rings out over the train's speakers. "Stand clear of the closing doors." The train lurches forward.

As he hits Play on the video he was looking for, Reed thinks he hears Olive talking to him about some debate topic, but when he glances up, she's grabbing her chewed-up pencil, then rolls her eyes at him as she starts writing in her notebook. Deciding she'll be occupied for a while, he returns to studying the play on the screen.

The train pulls out of the station, and the siblings, lost in their own worlds, sit quietly as it speeds through a tunnel to the next stop. "You've arrived at Nostrand Avenue," the scratchy female voice on the train announces. The doors swing open, and passengers begin to flood into the train. Seats fill up quickly, and some people are left to stand. It's a busy car, but it isn't full. The train doors close.

CHAPTER 2

A Mutual Network You Can't Escape

Martin Luther King Jr.

AS THE TRAIN PULLS OUT OF THE STATION, Reed notices some commotion behind him and briefly turns. *It appears some people jumped between the moving cars and are making their way through the crowd as if they are in a hurry.* Even though there's clearly a sign that states "Riding or moving between cars is prohibited unless there is an emergency, or as directed by police," people make their way through from time to time, so Reed pays it no mind. Instead, he turns his attention back to a screamer of a goal by one of his favorite players, Boyd Alexander.

Reed hears a distant *slap* as the door between the cars opens again, and based on the sound of conversation behind him, a few other people are making their way down the car and talking. *They're probably looking for their friends.*

He remains focused on his phone until several minutes later, when Reed becomes aware two people have stopped next to him and Olive.

"Hey, kid. Mind if we see your ID?" the first person asks, looking down at Reed.

As Reed looks up over the rim of his phone, his eyes catch a glimpse of dark blue pants. As his eyes move up farther, he sees the belt with a gun, mace, and other tools and realizes it's a police officer's belt. Cop! *What's going on?* he thinks.

The officer who spoke isn't too tall, but he is a little round and older, and as Reed looks up he notices he's also bald and has a beard streaked with a few gray hairs. The other officer looks like he just graduated high school. The younger officer's uniform is a little too crisp and spotless. He is clean cut with a baby face and perfectly combed hair. Both officers are White.

Reed puts his headphones in the front chest pocket of his jacket. He doesn't dare place his hands anywhere near his waist with the officers around, even to put something away. He hears his dad's voice: *Don't make any sudden moves, and make sure they can always see your hands.* He positions both feet flat on the floor, balances the soccer ball on his lap, and places his hands in plain sight, on top of the ball. "I'm sorry, Officers, how can I help you?" Reed replies, looking up at the men.

Reed sees Olive reach for her phone, and he knows what's going through her head because the same thing is going through his. Their dad always tells them it's important to record all interactions with police officers, just in case.

The police haven't done anything wrong. Maybe this is just a quick check and they'll move on. If that's the case, recording and deleting a video costs nothing. But if something does happen, they'll be glad Olive is recording. If she decided not to record the interaction, or if she were to miss a few seconds or minutes because she "didn't think anything would happen," that lapse could be the difference between the justice system believing Reed . . . or not. Reed knows that if it comes down to his word against the officers', he might not be believed. But a video doesn't lie.

Reed watches as Olive holds up her cell phone toward the officers and presses Record. She leans back a little so the camera can catch the officers standing inches from Reed, towering over him. With her other hand, she puts the notepad away and returns her half-chewed pencil back behind her ear, always keeping the camera focused on what's happening.

The officers are so close to Reed they are nearly standing on his toes. He looks down and slides his feet under his seat, narrowly avoiding being stepped on as the officers inch closer to him. He's completely boxed in, unable to get up or slide out of his seat even if he wanted to.

"C'mon, you heard my partner. Let's see it already. Get your ID out," the second officer says, pushing the older officer to the side and extending his hand for Reed's ID.

"Sir, I did not hear him. I apologize. May I ask why you need my ID for riding on the train?" Reed asks, pushing back politely like his dad taught him.

The older officer puts his hand up in front of the second one and looks at him as if to say, "Relax, I got this." He turns back to Reed, bends down a little, and asks again.

"Let's start over. My name is Officer John Bingham. And what I asked was, 'Do you mind if we see your ID, please?'" Officer Bingham repeats with the same welcoming smile.

"Respectfully, Officer . . ." Reed says as his voice cracks. He clears his throat. "Respectfully, Officer Bingham, I do mind, and I do not wish to give you my ID." The tone of his voice drops, getting a little softer and calmer.

"Where are you coming from?" the second, younger officer asks Reed from behind his partner.

Reed's heart skips a beat when the officer asks him that question. *Why are these officers randomly asking me questions? What's going on?* He can't stop worrying about what these officers want and how this conversation will end. Will he just be questioned and let go? Detained and frisked? Arrested? He tries to keep his face and body relaxed so he looks calm on the outside, but on the inside, his heart begins to beat harder and faster. He closes his eyes and takes a deep breath.

As he does, he remembers more of his dad's words. *If you think things are going badly while around cops, remember BAAD: Breathe. Assess. Act. Details. Breathe. Things will be moving very quickly. You're going to have a million thoughts racing through your head. You may be nervous, freaking out, or trying to answer questions or get away. But before you do anything, take a deep breath. Assess. What's the situation? Are you in a car? Walking down the street? Are you being questioned? You can't think of what you need to do unless you know what's going on. Act. What should you do? Every situation is different, but if you breathe and assess, you will know what combination of de-escalation and standing up for your rights is needed in that situation. Details. Try to remember as many details as possible because after the interaction is done, you may need to file a report. What is the officer's badge number? What intersection were you at? What was the time of day? All of these things will be important after the police are gone.*

Reed closes his eyes and takes another deep breath. Then he opens his eyes and looks back up at the young officer. The name tag on his vest shines like it's brand-new: Jefferies.

"I'm coming from school—actually, my sister's school, sir," Reed responds quickly and calmly corrects himself. He doesn't want to ignore the question. But he also makes sure to give no more information than the officer asked for.

"Oh, is that so? And where is the school?" Officer Jefferies presses mockingly, asking another question as if trying to catch Reed in a lie.

"It's just a few blocks away from the Utica subway station," Reed answers, hoping that giving the officer a little information will pacify him.

"Oh, is that MS 614?"

"No, sir. It's MS 416," Reed says, still trying to show no emotion.

The officer nods his head.

He knew that. He's trying to test me to see if I'm lying.

Officer Bingham confidently steps in. "Where are your friends? The ones you were walking the train with?"

Confused, Reed looks at Olive. She looks at him and shrugs her shoulders. Both of them tilt their heads toward each other and scrunch their eyebrows as if to say, "Huh?"

"Why the big rush? You know, it's not only a crime but also unsafe to walk between train cars when the train is moving. So, why'd you do it?" Officer Bingham continues.

"Officer, I'm sorry, but I don't know what you're talking about," Reed says, carefully moving his head from side to side. "I did not come onto the train with any friends.

I got on the train with my sister, into this exact train car, and sat down a couple stops ago. I don't know why you're asking me about walking through trains when I've been just sitting here with her," he pleads with the officers.

"Kid, don't worry. It's not a big deal." Officer Bingham chuckles as he stands up straight and adjusts his belt. "It's not like it's the crime of the century, ya know? And to be honest, I personally don't blame you." The officer leans closer to Reed as if he's about to tell Reed a secret, but instead he makes a sniffing noise while fanning his nose.

"We just came from the other train a second ago, and it stunk. Some homeless guy with a cart full of trash in there has some serious body odor. I would have walked out of that car as fast as I could too," Officer Bingham says with a grin as he stands back up, laughing with his partner.

The officers laugh to themselves for what seems like an awkwardly long time. They fan their noses in agreement as they look at each other.

Reed doesn't answer. *What's going on?* The officers' attempt at conversation is strange but seems oddly familiar, like when he can't remember the name of a song or its lyrics but can hum the melody.

Positive confrontation . . . shift blame . . . keep changing the subject whenever I try to tell them I did nothing wrong . . . Reed starts to think about how the officers are asking him questions. Then it clicks: this conversation seems way too familiar because it's just like something his dad taught him and Olive about talking with the cops. He finds his voice. "Officer, I'm really not trying to be difficult. But I don't know what you're talking about. I've only been here, in this train car, since we got on."

The officers pause again, as if trying to figure out what to do next. For a moment, they just stand there looking at Reed as he sits silently, waiting for them to ask another question or do something.

For a moment, Reed wonders if the silence is as awkward for the officers as it is for him.

"Kid, it's not that big of a deal," Officer Jefferies begins again. "We walked through the last car, and a few people said you were with a couple other boys who walked through that car behind us and into this car. Probably the same kids we saw smoking at the station you came from. And the description those people gave, you match it. Young Black male, dark hair, about five feet, nine inches tall. And to be honest, you kind of smell like you've been smoking weed too," he says, leaning into Reed. "But we aren't trying to get you in trouble if you work with us. So just tell us you did it, we'll give you a little warning, and we'll all get to move on with our days. You'll get to go home, and we'll go look for real criminals." The officer pauses. "But if you keep lying to us, it's going to get a lot worse for you. So, how are we going to handle this situation?"

Going to get a lot worse. The words echo in Reed's head as his heart skips again.

Breathe, Reed reminds himself. *They think I was with the other boys, the guys I saw at the station. Does my jacket smell like weed? What do I say? "I think you are talking about some guys I saw walking into the station"? Or "I didn't smoke, I was just talking to them"? If what I've told them isn't enough to make them stop accusing me of a crime, what good will explaining the truth do? Can I trust that they'll believe me? Will they turn the fact that I was with someone who committed a crime against me, even though I didn't commit one myself? Would the truth get me out of this situation or make it worse?*

The hair on the back of Reed's neck stands up. The officer has given him a choice that isn't a choice at all: either admit to a crime he didn't do or accept things will get worse.

But what does "worse" mean? Will he be arrested? Beaten? Jailed? Killed? If he admits to the crime, will it even make things better? It couldn't. *What should I do? What can I do? What's going to get me home safe?*

Officer Jefferies lets out an exaggerated sigh as he steps in front of Officer Bingham, pushing him to the side. He's clearly frustrated that the conversation is going nowhere fast.

"Hey! Kid! Let's get this moving. You know what you potheads did back at the last station. We know how kids like you like weed," Officer Jefferies says with a scoff.

And that's when Reed realizes what's really going on.

CHAPTER 3

When You Make Up Your Mind, Fear Diminishes

Rosa Parks

REID TECHNIQUE! Reed thinks. He can't believe he forgot the name of something so similar to his own name. It's a type of interrogation that a guy named Reid came up with in the '50s. A lot of police still think it's a helpful interrogation tool, but it has led to many false confessions, especially from teenagers. It's the same technique the police used when they interrogated the Central Park Five, a story Reed's dad has told him and his sister many times.

His dad's lessons echo in his head. *If an officer is asking you a bunch of questions—questions about where you're coming from, what you did or didn't do, things like that—and you didn't call the police or you're not making a report because something happened to you . . . They probably believe you committed a crime. If they are asking you questions and expecting a response, they aren't trying to "understand" what happened or "get both sides of the story," like they'll probably tell you they're trying to do. It's very likely that they suspect you are guilty, but they need you to confess to something or connect you to the crime. If you're ever having this kind of conversation with an officer, there's very little, if anything, you can say to that officer to change their mind. If they question you, make sure you understand the Reid technique.*

Reed feels his pulse begin to race. *They're asking me questions so they can arrest me! But I didn't do anything wrong. I didn't commit a crime.*

"We're not going to ask again: let us see your ID, kid," Officer Jefferies says, more forcefully than when Officer Bingham asked.

Reed nods in agreement as the officer holds out his hand. He recalls that the laws in every state are different. Some states require that you give your ID to an officer when they ask, while some states, depending on the situation, go so far as to say it's a crime *not* to give your ID to an officer when asked. New York falls into neither of those categories; New Yorkers are not required to give their IDs to officers when requested, but officers can detain anyone for as long as an investigation takes. In other words, the stop could last as long as the officer wants.

Reed considers that if the officers think he's working with them, they might be more likely to let him go. He doesn't want to be in this situation any longer than he needs to be. He glances at Olive. She's still recording. Her eyes squint in concentration as she watches. Reed says, "Officer, I have a school ID in my wallet. Would it be okay if I gave that to you?"

The officer furrows his brow. "You don't have a state ID?" He looks at Officer Bingham, who nods. "Okay, a school ID will do."

Reed opens his jacket so the officers can see his waist, then gestures to his front left pocket. "I keep my wallet in my front left pocket, sir. Is it okay if I grab my wallet and give you my ID?"

Officer Jefferies nods. "Go ahead, kid."

Reed doesn't get up. He doesn't want to stand and make the officers think he is a danger to them or that he will run. His body becomes rigid as he worries about every move he makes. He tries not to shake, not to fidget, not to move a single muscle unless he's told to or he asks first. It feels strange, that something as routine as reaching for his wallet can cause such anxiety.

It's awkward, but he narrates each of his movements with an "Is it okay if I . . ." as he goes through the process of stiffening his left leg so he can slide his wallet out of his pants. His voice shakes a little.

Reed slowly removes a bright yellow wallet from his

front left pants pocket. It's so bright, it's like seeing the sun for the first time in the morning. His dad has a rule about wallets for his kids: "They can't be black, brown, silver, or any color that could look like a gun or weapon," he's warned them time and time again. "If you pull your wallet out of your pants, jacket, purse, whatever, it has to be clear from a million miles away, even in the dark, that it's not a weapon." So Reed chose bright yellow.

Reed holds his wallet on his knee without opening it. Then his fingers pry the wallet open just enough to pull out his ID. Though he's still nervous, looking at his bright yellow wallet reminds Reed of his dad, and somehow, he feels a little safer.

The color wasn't the only rule Reed had when it came to his wallet. The other was where he was supposed to keep it. Reed's dad has told him to always keep his wallet in the same front left pants pocket. *A wallet in your front pocket, especially your left pocket, is about keeping your hands visible and being safe. Officers are trained to think that hands they can't see can kill.* If Reed kept his wallet in a back pocket, an officer could think that when he was reaching for his wallet behind him, he was instead reaching for something like a gun or a knife. If a reach looks too dangerous, it is too dangerous for Reed. And Reed knows officers can respond to potential danger with deadly force.

When Dad first told him about the "rules of the

wallet," Reed thought they were unfair, and he let his dad know. "Why do I have to do this? So I look like less of a threat? This is my responsibility, not theirs, to make sure they can tell what's in my hand before they act? So we all have to put our bright, ridiculously colored wallets in specific places to make police feel comfortable?!" His dad had listened to all of Reed's questions and then, with a slow shrug of the shoulders, simply said, "Yeah, it's unfair, but it may be what gets you home safe one day, and so that's why it's a rule."

"C'mon, kid! Let's hurry this along; we don't have all day," Officer Jefferies commands, rushing Reed along.

Reed doesn't want to open his wallet all the way and allow the officers to see inside it. He knows that everything the officers see on him or in his wallet can extend their investigation. That's why his ID is always in the front slip of his wallet, so he knows exactly where it is and can remove it easily. Dad often reminds them, "Less is always more when preparing for potential police interactions."

After sliding out his school ID, Reed simultaneously removes the card right next to it in his wallet: the one he and his dad made. Some public defenders' offices give their clients business cards that have "know your rights" info on the back, so Reed and his dad decided to make a card invoking his rights in case an officer ever stopped him. Their card includes Reed's and his parents' names on the front. It also has his parents' phone number. On the back, it says, "I do not wish to speak with you. I do not consent to being searched. I want my lawyer and my parents. I am not over eighteen years old." Reed starts to hand his "Invoke Your Rights" card and school ID to the first officer.

Officer Jefferies snatches them from Reed's hand. "Speak with your lawyer. Consent," the officer mumbles. "What's this, and why don't you have any state ID?" he asks, holding up Reed's two documents. The officer looks at the school ID a second time and then reexamines the homemade card, flipping it back and forth and reading either side.

"Oh, you're a freshman at Elijah McCoy High School. That's a really good school, isn't it?" the officer asks. "Are you there on a scholarship or something?" He sneers.

Reed sits there, silently fuming at the officer's biased assumptions. *What does he think—I'm not good enough, not smart enough, to go to school there?*

Reed looks over to check on Olive; she's still recording and watching everything. A part of him hopes she is getting everyone on camera and not cutting off someone's head or badge. She seems focused, trying to keep the camera on whoever is speaking. They both know police officers in New York can be recorded while they are doing official police business, so they aren't too worried about getting into any trouble. *Just keep recording, Olive,* Reed thinks. But another part worries about what they may say or do to her because she is recording. *Should I tell her to stop?*

Officer Jefferies examines Reed's ID then looks to Officer Bingham. "Hey, Bingham, I can't run his name in the system while the train is moving. We need to step off the train."

Step off the train? Reed just wants to get home. The last thing he wants is to get off the train and be taken somewhere by these police officers.

"I'm sorry, Officers, but why are you running his name in the system? We thought you were just asking us some questions," Olive says, her voice echoing through the train for the first time. Her tone is polite but firm. "Are we being detained now? Are we being arrested?" Reed turns to Olive, happy to hear a familiar confidence in his sister's voice.

Officer Bingham glances at Olive. "No, it's just protocol—for your safety and ours."

Reed knows they want to look to see if he has warrants or a record. Dad would call it a "fishing expedition." The officers aren't sure they are right, so they want to see if something incriminating can be found. Reed has no warrants, so on the one hand, he doesn't have to worry they'll find anything. But he also knows that if the officers are checking him for warrants, things have gotten past the point of talking things out.

As the officers talk to themselves about what to do

next, he looks over at Olive again and sees her recording with one hand; her other hand is clenched. Reed can't tell if she's nervous, anxious, frightened, or some jumbled mix of all three. He reaches down and grabs her clenched fist. He pries it open and holds it gently, hoping she will feel safe. Then he looks back at the officers and in a calm whisper says, "Officer, I am a minor and won't answer any questions without my parents and a lawyer, like the card I handed to you says. It has my parents' number on it so you can call. And my dad is my lawyer. I'm sorry, but he's told me that any time an officer tries to question me, I should give them the card and tell them exactly what I am telling you now. I do not consent to any searches. I will not speak until my lawyer is here."

Officer Jefferies rolls his eyes. "You can do whatever you want, big guy. But this is the deal—my partner and I saw a group of Black boys smoking weed back at the Utica subway stop. We chased them into the subway and onto this train. We walked through the train looking for you guys, and luckily, some of the passengers in the other car described what those boys looked like. They said one had a ball just like you've got on your lap. Don't know where your friends are, but you match the description. Plus, you've got your foot up on the seat like you own the place or something. So we are going to get off this train and talk about why you ran from the cops, walked through the trains, and when we first came into the car and approached, you had your feet up on the seat, which is a crime if you didn't know. But that talk isn't happening here, it's happening off the train."

The officers inch closer to Reed. "So we're getting up, right?" he asks softly, in a way that sends a chill down Reed's spine.

Thoughts tumble through his mind. *I wasn't smoking weed. I wasn't chased down any stairs. I didn't run through any train. What are you two thinking? This is crazy; you're just fishing for something.* He wants to ask, "And what's the description?" but he holds back. He knows the officers don't have to answer his questions. They can even lie to him if they want; it's completely legal. *I'm not talking my way out of this one; they've already made up their minds. Don't give an excuse, don't try to explain. Just answer their questions and try to end this whole thing as quickly as possible.*

The train announcement breaks the awkward silence. "This is Atlantic Avenue, Barclays Center."

"C'mon, big guy," Officer Jefferies says. He steps back from Reed and opens his body to the door. He gestures with his arm as if to say, "This way, please. Step off the train."

Never negotiate from a position of weakness, Reed remembers Dad saying. *You can't win your case arguing or fighting in the streets with these officers. The streets are where the cops have all the power. They have the power to harass you, to arrest you, and—in certain circumstances—to take your life without repercussion, and they know it. Collect the facts, don't give them—that's your role when interacting with police outside a court room. Only in court does your power with a cop become closer to equal. Not equal. Just closer to it. Don't you ever think about giving in or giving up. Because we don't do that in this family. We don't negotiate from a position of weakness.*

Reed decides, *This isn't where I fight. My strength is in not fighting them here, where they have the power.*

He stands up to get off the train.

CHAPTER 4

These Men Ask for Fairness and Only Fairness

Abraham Lincoln

AS REED STANDS UP, Olive gets up and steps back from the officers so the camera can see everyone as they walk off the train. As Reed collects his things, he and Olive lock eyes for a moment and silently communicate. Olive's eyes are determined and focused, as if to say, "Don't worry—I've got your back." Reed sees the strength in her expression; she's ready to push back. But he looks at Olive and silently asks her not to do anything. "I've got this," he says with his eyes.

A few passengers look at the officers with critical eyes as they pass. Officer Jeffries turns to the rest of the train and says in an official-sounding voice, "We are simply clearing some things up with this suspect. There's nothing to see here," as if he is protecting the people from Reed.

The train doors are wide open, and the young officer's foot is jammed in the threshold to keep them that way. People continue to exit and enter the train as Reed grabs his headphones from his jacket pocket.

"Can I give my headphones to my sister, please?" Reed asks the officers as he goes into his front jacket pocket.

Officer Bingham nods as if to say yes.

If he gets arrested, he doesn't want to take anything with him in case he doesn't get it back from the police. His cell phone, wallet, and keys are things he wants to take because those will help him get in touch with his family or get home if he gets the chance. He's also always sharing his location with his parents. So if he is brought to a precinct, they will know where he is because the police aren't always going to call his family to tell them.

Reed hands his headphones to Olive.

Reed can see Olive biting her lip; she knows what Reed is preparing for. Reed senses she's been staying quiet so she doesn't get in any trouble with the officers herself, but it's clear she can't hold back anymore. Just then she blurts out, "Taking up more than one seat?" Olive asks politely, but there's a frustrated edge to the words. "I'm sorry, sir," she quickly adds, "but there is a homeless guy sleeping over there." She points down the car. "This woman has her shopping bags next to her." Olive gestures to the person across from her. "And that guy is man spreading so hard he's taking up three seats." Olive points to a man at the other end of the train. The politeness in her voice is slowly beginning to fade.

The man-spreader closes his legs as people on the train begin to stare at him. Olive continues. "And of all the people you could choose to stop, you pick the high school freshman who graduated on the honor roll in middle school and coaches five-year-old rec soccer? He has no record; he's just a kid. I'm just a kid. What are you looking for in his record? And even if my brother was using too many seats, you could just write him a ticket and be on your way. In New York, a stop should only last as long as it takes to investigate a crime. So please let us be. This is an illegal stop."

Reed doesn't know whether to feel proud of his sister or scared for her safety.

The officers look at Olive with blank stares, as if to ask, "You done?" Officer Jefferies looks back at Reed. "We're just going to talk. You're the one who's been talking all this 'I don't consent, I want a lawyer' nonsense. We didn't say anything about arresting you or searching you. What, you got some weed on you? Don't worry, it's barely a crime these days. We don't care. We don't arrest anyone for that anymore. We guessed you had weed on you anyway from the looks of you. If you give it to us now, it's not a big deal," the officer says, extending his hand toward Reed while continuing to stand in the open doorway.

Reed hates how wrong the officer is. He wants to argue, to put him in his place for all the ridiculous things he's saying, like that he doesn't need to ask for a lawyer or that he should just talk to them. Not to mention his false accusations that Reed walked through a train when it was moving and was with the group of boys, who sound like they committed some crimes. Nothing the officer has said is right. Admitting to a small crime wouldn't lead to Reed getting a warning. Especially since having weed at his age is a crime. He'd get a ticket or worse, for something he didn't even have. How would he explain that he admitted to a crime that he didn't commit just to get out of being questioned? Who would believe him?

But Reed holds his tongue; he doesn't spit out the first thing he wants to say. It feels like the cops are just telling lies to get him to argue with them. *That's exactly what they want me to do—keep talking*, Reed thinks. He feels pressured to speak. But he knows that the more he feels pressured to give up his right to remain silent, the tighter he should hold on to it. So he says nothing, puts his ball under his arm, and turns toward the door. And as he does, he looks up and sees everyone on the train staring back at him.

This whole time, his focus has been on the officers. But now he realizes that there have been a lot of eyes on him. Behind those eyes, he sees disgust, anger, shame, fear, and hope. A few people yell at the officer, saying things like "He's just a kid," and "He didn't do anything wrong!" Many turn their heads, burying their faces in books or looking to their cell phones as they readjust their headphones. Any excuse to not have to look Reed in the eyes.

The doors of the train begin to close on Officer Jefferies, but he leans his back against one of the doors and stiff-arms the other, keeping them from closing. "Stand clear of the closing door," the automated voice announces. Officer Jefferies sticks his head out and waves to the conductor down the platform. He screams, "NYPD! Hold the train! NYPD!" and sticks his chest out the train, pointing to his badge.

People on the train groan at the delay.

Reed gets up and takes a step toward the door. He pats his pockets and looks down, as if he's forgotten something, and looks back at his seat to see what it could be. "Today! You may not be in a hurry, but some of us have homes and families to get back to tonight," Officer Jefferies says.

"My soccer ball, duh," he says under his breath, remembering what he's missing. He turns to see his ball rolling back and forth on the subway seat. For just a second, Reed forgets where he is. Because in that second, when he sees his ball, he takes a step to grab it. He forgets to ask the cop if he can get it, forgets to narrate what he's doing. Forgets that he is with a cop who is questioning him about a crime and is telling him to get off the train. For only a second, he is a fourteen-year-old boy just trying to get his ball back. And as he takes a step toward the ball to get it, Reed is lifted off his feet by the collar of his shirt, which squeezes into his throat.

"Hey! He's trying to run!" He hears screaming behind him as he chokes and gasps for air. He's being pulled, pulled off the train by the officer grabbing his collar.

A couple people on the train pull out their cell phones to record Reed and the officers. One woman stands from her seat and screams at the officers, "What are you doing to these children?! They were just sitting here, doing nothing wrong the whole time. I saw them walk on the train together."

"Ma'am, we are in the middle of an investigation. Please step back—we will be done soon." The train ignites as other passengers begin to yell at the officers.

"It wasn't them. It was the boys in the other car." The voice pierces through the crowd, but the officers pay it no mind. The train becomes agitated as the yelling and shouting escalates.

"Leave the kids alone!"

"Just get off the train already!"

"You're being racist! Stop targeting Black kids!"

"Why is this taking so long? Just get them off the

train already! These thugs are always causing delays for no reason!"

The voices continue, growing in frustration and anger.

Reed wants to be anywhere but here. *Is this my fault?* Reed has always been taught to be proud of himself, to be kind, to do good. Now, looking at the crowd, he can't help but wonder, *Did I do something wrong? But what could I have possibly done wrong? Is something wrong with me? Am I the reason these people are angry? Am I going home today?*

As Reed is forced toward the train door, Officer Jefferies lets go of Reed's collar and grabs him by the upper arm. Reed holds his throat as he gasps for air. His collar, stretched out by the officer's clasp, hangs low below his chin. Between coughs, Reed can hear Officer Jefferies yell, "Hurry up! Get off the—"

Reed shouts as he tries to shake off the officer. "You don't have the right to grab me like that! What are you doing?" But the officer's hands just clamp tighter around Reed's arm.

"Stop tensing up, kid. That isn't going to work out. Relax. Relax," the officer says, continuing to hold Reed by the arm.

"I'm not doing anything. Stop grabbing me!" The officer squeezes Reed's arm harder and harder as he pulls Reed into the doorway. "Stop messing around; it won't be good for you if you don't stop."

Reed's backpack and arm flail in the air. "Please! Don't put your hands on me, sir. I do not want to be touched by you, and I don't consent to being touched! Frisked! Searched! Anything!" Reed says, sending the other officer a pleading look. But Officer Bingham continues to stand aside, doing little.

Officer Jefferies loosens his grip as Reed is thrown from the train. Reed feels a sharp pop in his left shoulder and screams out in pain. He stumbles and barely catches himself from falling on the platform. As Reed is whipped around, all he sees is a wall coming closer and closer.

But before he crashes into the wall, Officer Jefferies grabs his arm again, this time bending it at the elbow and pressing it against Reed's back. But while twisting his arm, he slams him into the wall.

CHAPTER 5

It's Not Your Inferiority, It's Their Inhumanity

James Baldwin

OFFICER JEFFERIES PULLS Reed's arm higher and higher up his back. Reed knows these officers are about to arrest him. *There's no talking back or fighting back now,* Reed thinks. The officer tries to force Reed to the ground by bear-hugging him, pinning his arms to his side as someone else tries to handcuff him. Reed feels two more hands grab his right arm and two other hands grab his left.

Wait, how many people is that? There seem to be more than just the two officers who interrogated Reed on the train.

But not long after the thought flits through his mind, his body is pulled away from the wall and then slammed

43

back into it. The last time Reed weighed himself, he was 130 pounds, but he's getting pushed and pulled like he weighs nothing.

"Stop resisting! Stop resisting! *Stop resisting!*" Reed's ears ring as one of the officers next to him yells over and over again—an officer he's never heard before. A second voice joins the first. "*Stop resisting!*" As Reed is swarmed, he can't tell what's happening. His weightless body is being tossed back and forth as his eyes clench harder with every scream in his ear.

"I'm innocent! I'm innocent! I did not walk through the train. It wasn't me!" Reed screams, or at least he thinks he does, but his tongue is gripped with fear. As his mind races, his dad's lessons somehow ring in his ear. *If you ever get arrested, you'll probably be more scared than you've ever been in your life. But you've gotta do your best to stay calm because it could mean the difference between you coming home or not. If you act out of fear or anger, it won't matter how right or how wrong they are—that may not end well for you. So, as hard as it may be, you have to stay calm. Don't pick a fight with these people—not with your words and not with your body. Because those cops have way too much power over your body in that moment, right or wrong, and that's a fight you've got to come home safe from. That's the goal. That's your only goal. Come home safe.*

With the officers' shrieks of "Stop resisting!" still ringing in his ears, Reed battles against his instincts to fight back, his instincts to try to get free. *Anything and every-thing is resisting,* Reed remembers his dad telling him. *Resisting could be you walking away when they ask to "talk to you," it could be you talking back, it could be something as simple as you saying no. It just depends on the cop. Don't think that resisting only means fighting back. The reason this is so important to know is that when you resist, it allows them to take you anywhere they want to take you. They can take you up against a wall, can take you to the ground, can take you away from us. It could lead to you getting punched and kicked, arrested, or worse. So when I say, "Don't resist," understand what that really means.*

"Step back, miss!" Officer Bingham commands. Reed's eyes fly open to see what's going on, then he realizes the officer is talking to a terrified Olive. Reed gets a glance of the fear in her eyes as he is thrown back into the wall.

"He's going to be okay. Just step back!" Officer Bingham continues. "But, miss, you can't record us. Put your phone away."

Olive's voice cracks, then trembles. "I'm s-s-so sorry, but Officer, that's not the rule or the law." She takes a deep breath. "I have the right to lawfully observe and record police activities, like detaining or arresting a person, so long as I'm in a public area or a place I'm allowed to be. You're not allowed to stop me—or try to stop me—from recording. You can't discourage me, intimidate me, or tell me to stop. This is not a crime. This is my right!"

Olive says firmly, holding her phone up. The officer drops his hand as she places the camera on him.

"Then you need to step back, miss," Officer Bingham says, dropping his voice.

Olive takes a small step back. She keeps her phone on Reed.

"I'm not resisting! I do not consent! I'm not resisting!" Reed keeps saying over and over again.

"Sit down."

"Put your hands up."

"Put your hands behind your back."

The officers give different instructions as they push and pull him into place. He tries to breathe and think about what's happening and do as they ask. *Do I sit, stand? Where do I put my hands? What do they want me to do?* But he quickly realizes it's one thing to talk about this kind of situation in the safety of his home and another thing to live it, fearful of what might happen next.

The struggle lasts for seconds, but it feels like an hour. Officer Jefferies sweeps Reed's legs. He feels himself drop to the ground, shoulder first as two officers fall on him too. He quickly rolls to his stomach, trying to put his hands behind his back. "The quicker I put my hands in place, the less they'll hurt me," Reed says to himself, hoping for the best.

Officer Jefferies gets on top of Reed and drives a knee into his back. Reed screams out in pain. But his scream is cut short as he gasps for air when the officer puts more weight behind his knee. The officers bend Reed's arms in all different directions. When they bend an arm the wrong way, he stiffens in pain, so they bend it even more. *Give up*, runs through his mind. His shoulder throbbing in pain, he tries his best to let his arms go limp so the officers can move them where they want.

Let them arrest you. Over and over again, he negotiates with his body not to freak out, not to push back, not to tense up. But with every twist and pull, he pulls back in agony. Every bit of him wants to escape, to get away. He's terrified and hurting. Though he knows what will happen if he tries. So he fights his own instincts. *Don't run. Don't fight. Give in.*

Dad's words float into his mind. *If you are ever in a situation where you're being arrested, don't fight. Let them arrest you.* Another jolt of pain rides down Reed's arm. *You're not giving up or giving in to the cop. It's about not letting them take. Take your liberties, take your freedom, take your life. It's about you exercising your power, as little as it may be in the streets, and exercising it to the fullest. You are being powerful in that moment, not weak.* Reed tries to hold these words tightly, to convince his body that these lessons are true.

Reed lies there, motionless but tense, while the two officers continue to pin his arms behind his back. Officer Jefferies's knee is still digging into Reed's back.

Son, Reed recalls his dad telling him in a soft, shaking voice, *every day, I put on a suit and fight for the rights of those who cannot afford an attorney. Most of the time they aren't harmed by the police when they are arrested. But sometimes they experience abuse in a way that may affect you too. A way that I may not be able to shield you from. Not every cop is going to treat you with the respect and dignity you deserve. But if cops do approach you, if they choose to question you, this is what I need you to do. Stand tall when they ask you a question. Answer them directly. Say, "Yes, sir," or "Yes, ma'am," when they speak to you. Never give more information than they ask, and know your rights. These are the things I've always taught you. But here's one last lesson: There may come a time when a decision needs to be made. Your rights or your life. I hope you never have to make this choice, but if you do, I need you to choose your life. Choose your life each and every time. No matter how right you may be or how wrong they are, if you believe your life is in danger from a cop, I need you to give in. I'd rather fight for my son in court than fight for his memory. I pray you never have to face a situation like this, but I need you to promise me that if you are ever around a cop and you fear for your life, you'll give in.*

I promise, Dad, Reed thinks to himself now, and his body finally relaxes.

An officer clamps the handcuffs on his wrists, then squeezes them tight. He tightens the cuffs more and more, cutting into Reed's wrists. Reed has seen handcuffs before. At court with his dad, he's noticed the correction officers have handcuffs on their hips. He's also seen his dad's clients wearing them during court appearances. He's held a pair of handcuffs before, felt how heavy they are. But the bite of steel cutting into his skin is something he's never known.

One by one, the cops climb off Reed's back. Officer Jefferies is last, and Reed feels air return to his lungs as the immense weight and pressure is removed. An officer pulls Reed up to his feet by the handcuffs' chain. Reed's hands rise behind him till his shoulders won't bend anymore and his body is lifted off the ground, his arms stretched like the handles of a heavy plastic bag full of groceries, just about to rip. He clenches his teeth in pain as the officer twists his arms behind him. Reed looks up and sees four, five, maybe six officers—and just behind them, a terrified Olive. Reed looks past the police uniforms. All he can focus on is his sister, who is shaking and still holding up her cell phone.

The handcuffs are tight. The skin around the cuffs now burns.

"Spread your legs," a voice shouts, interrupting Reed's thoughts. Reed spreads them open. "More!" the voice commands, and this time Reed can feel the officer's feet kicking the insides of his ankles, pushing them farther and farther apart to open his legs.

Reed's legs, his arms, his body are no longer his. He has to move, stand, and hold himself however Officer Jefferies and the other cops want him to. Reed no longer feels like the proud young man his parents taught him to be but like a puppet, a plaything that the officers can push and pull as they want. "Do you have anything on you that you're not supposed to have? Do you have anything on you that can prick or cut me?" Officer Jefferies asks as he pats Reed down, starting from the ankles. He looks down Reed's shoes and up his pant sleeves. His hands move up the outside and then the inside of Reed's legs. Reed turns his head to the side to see what's happening. He notices people on the platform looking at him.

"I wonder what he did?"

"Ugh. This is why the train was stopped?"

"Another one."

Reed can hear their judgmental comments and read their expressions of disgust.

"Cell phone, keys, and . . . wallet," Officer Jefferies says, listing the contents of Reed's pockets as he hands the items to another officer. The officer places Reed's things on the bench next to him, then pats down Reed's jacket, pulling out a perfectly folded piece of paper from one of the pockets.

"Elijah McCoy High School soccer tryouts?" the officer says, puzzled, as he reads the permission form. He balls up the paper and tosses it next to a nearby trash can. Reed watches as the paper bounces off the wall and rolls behind the can. *My sign-up sheet for the varsity team. I need that to try out tomorrow.* But the world of soccer tryouts seems so far away, almost unreal. How did today go from tryouts to getting arrested?

Officer Jefferies checks Reed's chest, under his arms, and back. He doesn't miss any part of Reed's body. "All clear," Officer Jefferies tells the other officers as he gives Reed one final push against the wall, face first.

CHAPTER 6

Ignorance Allied With Power Is The Most Ferocious Enemy of Justice

James Baldwin

THEIR SEARCH OVER, the officers spin Reed around to face them and push him backward against the wall. Four officers surround Reed. He doesn't move or say anything. He simply watches as the officers collect themselves after fighting to handcuff a teenager.

"You good?" one officer asks another.

"Yeah, I'm all right. My knee is a little banged up, but I'll live."

The officers laugh and pat one another on the back, proud of what they've accomplished. Reed imagines they must be thinking, *We got our man.*

No one checks on Reed. No one asks about the pain in his shoulder, the ringing in his ear, or the absolute terror he feels. The officers just leave him there, leaning against the wall. He is a discarded thing they are done playing with, done pushing around.

Officer Bingham stands between Olive and the other officers as if she is some danger to them all. As if this little girl could stop them from throwing Reed's body up and down the subway platform.

"Miss, he is going to be okay. If he complies with us and he has no warrants, we will let him go," Reed hears Officer Bingham tell Olive.

Reed looks at his sister. Tears are running down her face. She doesn't appear as though she's heard a word Officer Bingham is saying. She stands there, biting her lip and clenching her fist, still doing the one thing she can do: recording what is going on.

Officer Jefferies puts his hand on Reed's shoulder. "So you wanted to do this the hard way? Guess we are going to be here for a while then. You better sit down."

Reed stays standing, silently protesting. "Sit!" Officer Jefferies commands, forcing Reed downward by his aching shoulder. Reed's knees buckle under the officer's hand, and he sits on the platform floor. Olive keeps recording the officers, struggling to see over their shoulders as she tries to catch everything that is happening to Reed.

Slouched on the dirty subway floor, Reed sits on

fast-food wrappers and bottles. He, too, looks like something that's been thrown away.

"Officer, can you at least let him sit on the bench, please!" Olive yells, pointing at the bench mere feet from Reed. She looks petrified in fear. Her hand is over her mouth, and she's fighting back tears.

"It's okay," Reed's voice squeaks out. "I'm all right," he tries to reassure her, even though he's still scared himself.

Officer Bingham seems to be the only one who hears her. He turns and pushes through the officers.

"Here, son," he says, as he gently lifts Reed to his feet. Trash and dust cling to Reed's clothes as he is placed on the subway bench. Reed's left shoulder hangs lower than his right. He cringes with pain as he sits down.

This is defeat. He knows what losing feels like—he's lost soccer games before and he takes it pretty seriously. Whenever he loses a game, he feels as though it's his fault, even though he's just one of eleven players on the field. And the weight of each loss radiates in the way he sits, the way he frowns, the way he shuts down from the outside world. After a bad game, he usually gets really quiet, responding with just one-word answers. "Yes." "No." "Please." "Thanks." That's where he goes, that's what he feels, as he sits there. Defeated.

He is physically present but mentally . . . miles away.

Officer Bingham dusts Reed off, and a piece of trash falls from his pants. "You okay, son? Are the cuffs too tight?"

Reed understands this officer is trying to be nice, but he wants nothing to do with any of them after what they did to him. So he continues to sit in silent protest. He can feel the handcuffs biting into his wrists. No matter how nice one officer may be now, in Reed's mind, all of them either roughed him up or let it happen.

"Thanks for the help, guys," Officer Jefferies says, out of breath, as he grins at the other officers. "The kid tried to run off on us."

Three new officers arrive on the scene, including an olive-skinned woman about the same age as Reed and Olive's mom. Officer Jefferies straightens up and stands a little taller while he addresses her.

"Sergeant, we followed a group of teens from the Utica station onto the train. They were smoking marijuana. We could smell it as we chased them into the subway," he spits out quickly, explaining what was going on.

"Did you recover any marijuana from this kid or find any in the subway?" the sergeant asks, looking at Reed.

"No, we didn't find anything, but he did have about twenty-two dollars in cash on him, which is probably buy money from selling weed. And no, we didn't recover any marijuana at the scene—we were too busy trying to catch the kids. We lost track of them when they ran into the station and jumped the turnstile. They sprinted toward the train, and we got on just before the train left," Officer Jefferies explains.

"And you think these kids are the ones you saw? But it's a boy and a girl . . . What'd they look like?" the sergeant asks, again looking at Reed on the bench and then glancing over at Olive, who is still recording.

"There were maybe three to four Black males. We weren't close enough to them to get a good look, but we could see what they were wearing. Two of the boys had shortish hair. Couldn't tell with the others; one or two had hoodies on, I think, I couldn't really see their faces. A couple of them were wearing blue—they looked like they had matching track jackets. At least one was wearing shorts, and another was in jeans. We radioed in the descriptions of the boys just before we got on the train," Jefferies says.

The sergeant looks Reed up and down with a confused face, taking in his outfit, seeing he looks nothing like the description.

"So we just searched the train, looking for them. The passengers told us a few boys matching the description were walking between train cars to avoid us," Officer Jefferies continues.

One of the new officers on the scene looks down at Reed and asks, "What's your name, kid?" But Reed doesn't answer; he just sits there, slouching on the bench, head held low, lost in his thoughts.

"And was this kid one of them?" the sergeant asks.

"We believe so. We tried asking him questions, and he

didn't comply. Then he tried to run from us again. So we had to take him out of the—" Officer Jefferies is interrupted by the buzzing radios on the officers' shoulders.

"We have three at the Franklin Ave–Medgar Evers train stop suspected of fare beating," the voice over the radio says. Reed looks to the officers. He's terrified at first, but then he starts to feel hopeful.

He sees Olive standing close by and nodding. *She's probably thinking the same thing I am.* He notices Olive stop recording and put her phone to her head, then pull it down and frantically type. *Mom or Dad must not be answering his phone.* More hope flickers in Reed as he thinks, *Dad could be here soon.*

Olive finishes typing and points her phone back at the officers.

"Three Black males, ages fourteen to sixteen," the radio voice screeches.

"Hold on, guys, stay here with the kid," the sergeant says to the officers as she takes a step away and leans into her radio, listening closely to the scratchy voice. She leans her head to the radio, and Reed can tell she's talking to someone, but she's too far away for him to make out what she's saying.

The third new officer bends down and tries to speak with Reed. "Hey, kid, I'm Officer Pauli Murray. How's the shoulder? It looks a little banged up. Can you tell me what happened here?"

"Sore," Reed says under his breath. He looks up to see a young female officer. She seems to genuinely want to know what happened. "Officer, I'm not trying to be rude, but I already tried to tell those two what happened. I do not want to speak to anyone until I can talk to my lawyer. I want my lawyer."

"Officer, please, you have the wrong person," Olive says, advocating for Reed. "We weren't ever running between cars; we sat down once we got on. It's just my brother and me, no other boys. Ma'am, we were just minding our own business, and out of nowhere these officers came walking through the train and accused my brother of these random crimes. They tried to interrogate him. Tried to have him admit that he did something wrong when he never did. Then when they didn't get what they wanted, they threw him to the ground and handcuffed him! He didn't do anything wrong! We didn't do anything wrong. We just want to get home, Officer. Please!"

Reed looks at Olive, and in that moment he doesn't see the goofy, nerdy, sometimes annoying little sister he loves. Instead, he sees a young woman filled with determination and composure.

The sergeant returns with a puzzled look on her face. Olive turns her camera toward her, trying to capture everything that is happening as she walks closer to the officers and Reed.

"Step back, please," Officer Bingham tells her again.

"You can't be that close." Reed sees Olive quickly step back so as not to get in the officers' way. Their dad warned them about this too. *Even getting in a police officer's way can get you arrested. Resisting arrest, obstruction of governmental administration, and disorderly conduct are the three big ones they can use.* Reed knows these charges bother his dad the most. "Do as I say or get locked up" is how he describes cases where officers arrest people for not following orders. "Happens more than you think," he would say.

Don't push their buttons, Olive. Don't give them a reason to start questioning you or put you in cuffs. Even though there's no magic distance she has to stay away from the cops, Reed knows that the farther she can stand back, the better. "More!" the officer commands. Olive quickly takes a couple steps back again.

The sergeant turns to Officer Bingham. "Three Black juveniles, ages fourteen to sixteen, two wearing matching blue track suits, and one in a white-and-blue hoodie, short Caesar haircuts. Is that the perp description you were following?"

"Yeah, that was what we called in once we got on the train," Officer Bingham responds.

"Well, they arrested them two subway stops back, so it's not this kid. Do we have anything else on him?" the sergeant asks, sounding somewhat annoyed.

Officer Jefferies shakes his head and mumbles, "Nothing came up when we checked his name for warrants and he just had the buy money." He flips Reed's ID over, seeming unsatisfied with what he has seen.

"All right, cut him loose," the sergeant says.

"C'mon, kid. Time to go. You heard the sergeant," Officer Jefferies says, waving at Reed to stand up.

He slowly stands, grimacing in pain from his shoulder and wrists. The officer turns Reed around and uncuffs him. The metal chafes his wrists as the officer struggles to get them off. Once off, Reed rubs his wrists, trying to soothe the bite the handcuffs left behind.

Officer Bingham nods toward Reed's things next to him as he says, "Don't forget your things, kid." Reed turns to his left and begins to pick up his stuff. *Cell phone, keys, wallet,* mentally checking to make sure he has all of his things as he picks them up.

"All right kid, here's your ID. You're free to go," Officer Jefferies tells him.

Reed reaches out and takes his ID. He grabs his cards just as the officer releases them and they almost hit the ground. "This could've been handled so much easier, you know? We could have cleared this up if you just did what we asked you to do. I don't get why you people just don't listen; we aren't out here to hurt you or anything. Next time, just do what we ask, all right? Would save us all the headache of having to go through this," Officer Jefferies tells Reed as he puts his handcuffs back on his belt.

The officers walk away.

CHAPTER 7

Where You See Wrong or Injustice, Speak Out Because This Is Your Country

Thurgood Marshall

REED OPENS UP HIS WALLET and slides his ID back in the front, as always. Then he slides his wallet back into his front left pocket. He brushes a few pieces of trash off his pants and picks up his bag, silent the entire time. He steps toward the tracks as he hears the train approaching from down the tunnel. Then, barely audible, he says to Olive, "C'mon, train's coming."

"Wait!" Olive shouts out to the officers, phone still recording in her hand. "Can we have your police business cards with your names, precincts, and badge numbers, please?" she says softly but firmly.

Officer Jefferies is the first to walk back toward her. "Don't worry about it. There was no real arrest, so no report is going to be made. You don't need our info for anything. Like I said, we just had to question him. There doesn't need to be any paperwork on this. You guys are free to go." He grins at Olive like the two of them are old friends. "Listen, the train is coming." He points to the darkened subway tunnel that's slowly becoming brighter as a train begins to pull in.

"Officer, I'm not asking about an arrest. I'm sorry, it's just my parents told me to always ask for an officer's card whenever we have an interaction with one, and I don't want to go home and tell them I didn't even ask. Aren't you supposed to give one anytime a person asks?" Olive says, her politeness unwavering.

Officer Bingham walks up and hands his card to Olive, as do the other officers and the sergeant. Sergeant Douglas, Officer Lewis, Officer James, Officer Murray, Officer Greene. Olive reads the names out loud as she holds the cards in front of her camera.

Officer Jefferies walks up to Olive and pats his pockets like he's looking for something. "Well, I don't have cards on me. Here's my badge number," he says, leaning into Olive with his chest. "I can see you're recording." He chuckles as he points to his badge.

"Olive, let's just go home," Reed whispers, feeling exhausted.

Olive takes the cards and puts them in her pocket, turns off her camera, and walks over to Reed. "Hey, you good?" she asks as she attempts to hug him. But Reed steps back, not wanting to be touched.

"We are just a stop away from home. Let's go," he says under his breath.

"Did that really just happen?" Olive shouts, no longer frozen in her shock. "Did that really just happen to you? You were handcuffed basically because you matched the 'description'!" she says, making air quotes with her fingers. "That was crazy, right?" Olive keeps going on about how shocked she is, how they should do something. But Reed tunes her out. He rolls the Invoke Your Rights card between his fingers as a new train pulls up to the station.

"Reed? We have to make sure they don't get away with what they did to you and also make sure they don't continue to do this to others. We have to do something, Reed!" Olive pleads, but Reed doesn't respond; he just stares down at his card.

The train pulls in. Olive jumps into the train car, still talking to Reed, but he doesn't hear her. His hand falls to his side. He drops the Invoke Your Rights card on the platform as he steps onto the train. *I don't need this, so what's the point.* The doors close, and the train takes off, leaving his card behind.

Olive jumps into an empty seat by the door, but Reed doesn't sit this time. Instead, he puts his back to the closed door as he looks up and down the train car, scanning to make sure it's safe. The train speeds off to the next stop.

"This is Nevins Street," the subway announcement chimes as the train pulls in. "C'mon, let's go," Reed says as he steps out of the train. Olive tries to scribble one last word in her notepad as she rushes through the train door. They get off the train and walk out the subway.

Home isn't too far now, just a couple of blocks. Olive seems to have gotten the hint that Reed doesn't want to talk, so they walk home in silence.

Reed sees Olive scribbling in her notebook each time they wait at a street corner to cross. He doesn't say anything, but he can guess that she must be writing down what happened in hopes that maybe, just maybe, what she notes, what she remembers of what just happened, could help in reporting those cops. That these notes, along with her video, could bring some "justice," as she would probably call it, to the situation. But Reed is uninterested. He doesn't think what she's doing will do or change anything. Everything already happened, and no notes, no argument, nothing Olive has to offer can change that.

I could have really been hurt . . . they could have messed me up, Reed thinks as he feels a sharp pain in his shoulder. He pauses for a moment. *But they did hurt me!*

What if it had been worse? What if that call hadn't come through saying they arrested the other boys? One minute I was just hanging out, watching videos on the train . . . and the next I was handcuffed and thrown up against the wall! Why me? What did I do wrong?

The siblings walk up the street in silence, but Reed's mind races, thinking about all that could have happened, while Olive snatches moments from the walk to scribble in her notebook as fast as she can.

When Reed and Olive reach home, he rummages through his pockets, looking for the keys to the front door as he walks up the stairs. *Where are my keys? Did I lose them at the station?*

"Reed, I get that you're worried," Olive says, breaking the long silence. "Maybe you were even scared. I know I was. But why didn't you stand up for yourself like Mom and Dad taught us? The cops gave that garbage excuse you matched the description of some Black kids, basically, which was an absolute lie. I guess for once the way you dress is helpful; no one is wearing high-tops and an old man's blazer at your age," she says, trying to break the tension and get Reed to smile. But he doesn't respond. "If I were you, I would have said something. I know we can't fight back, but we can at least stand up for our rights. That cop grabbed you so hard; I swear your arm was going to come off! They jumped you! Like, actually jumped! Reed, that was excessive force, don't you think? Reed?"

Reed ignores her as he searches for the right key to open the door. He's been so desperate to get home for so long, and now he can't even find his keys!

"Reed, we should do something about this, don't you think?" she says again. "If we don't, they could do that to more people, and that's wrong. You got hurt! What if something worse happened? What if worse happens to the next kid they stop? Reed? *Reed?*" Olive asks. She tugs at the sleeve of his jacket.

"Drop it, Olive! I don't want to talk about it!" Reed snaps as he pulls his arm from Olive, takes out his keys, and puts the key in the front door. When he turns to her, he sees the shock on her face. His eyes must be bright red from crying. *I guess I look a lot worse than I thought.*

He turns away, hiding his face as he rushes through the doorway. Olive pushes open the door fully and slowly walks inside, locking the door behind her.

"Reed . . . you okay?" she asks. "It's going to be okay. You're going to be okay. Come look at the video with me. We can talk to Dad about it and see what he thinks," Olive says softly. She follows Reed as he walks through the first floor.

"Dad! We're home!" Olive shouts, but no one answers.

Reed's just glad Dad isn't there. He's never wanted to be alone so badly.

"I've got it!" Olive proclaims. "We can sue the NYPD and the officers. Like a civil rights case where we show your rights were violated. I have what happened on my phone. The time and place it happened, the officers' names." Olive holds up her cell phone. "I think we can really make a difference here. Maybe even make sure this doesn't happen to anyone ever again. But we have to move quickly. I think we have like ninety days to start a lawsuit."

Reed slowly opens his bedroom door, takes a deep breath, and looks back at his sister. "Olive, I know you're trying to help. And I really appreciate it—I do. But I just want to be left alone. Just drop it, okay?" Reed says, head hung low as he slides into his room and closes the door behind him.

"But Reed . . ." Olive says as the door closes right in front of her. She leans her head on Reed's door. "I just want to help."

Then, on the other side of the house, the front door opens. "Olive! Reed! Where are you?!" their dad calls.

CHAPTER 8

It Must Be Faced To Be Changed

James Baldwin

REED SITS ON THE EDGE OF HIS BED. He can hear Olive and his dad speaking in hushed tones outside his door. But he doesn't go to them. Even though he was longing for Dad at the subway station, he now can't bring himself to open the door.

Finally, there's a soft knock. "Reed?" Dad's voice is gentle, even hesitant.

Reed doesn't answer.

He knocks again. And again, Reed doesn't answer.

"Reed, I'm coming in. That okay?"

Reed stays silent and turns to open his backpack, taking things out and putting them away, trying to create some kind of order to reduce the chaos in his brain.

Dad slowly cracks open the door and sticks his head inside. Reed busies himself arranging his homework on his desk.

"Reed?" his dad says.

Reed stays silent. Words feel out of his reach.

"Reed, is everything okay?"

But Reed doesn't say anything.

He walks past his dad to the closet to hang up his jacket, then stands in front of the mirror on the back of his bedroom door as he unbuttons his dress shirt.

"Why me? Why?" Reed asks his reflection, as if it can answer. "I know . . . I know you all say I dress a little different. I hear the jokes some people make, and I don't care. I love the way I dress. I'm just not that kind of guy. I'm a straight-A student athlete. I volunteer at the soup kitchen every Easter. That's who I am . . . not the person they treated me like! They didn't see me or hear me. So who did they see? Like, what could I have done differently? Just let them frisk me, search me, arrest me till they figured out what was what? Why should I have to give up so much of my dignity to make their job easier, to make them feel safe around me?" He turns to his dad, looking for an answer.

Reed's dad steps into the room and closes the door behind him. He then exhales long and slow; he fidgets with his hands as his head hangs low, shaking. The strong and confident man who always seems to have all the answers looks worried and confused as he stares at the floor.

Dad finally looks up. "I'm sorry, Son, but I don't have the answers. I don't know if anyone does. But maybe if we talk about what happened, I can help, and we can figure out the answers together." Dad sits on the bed and pats the place next to him.

"I don't want to sit," Reed says as he empties his school bag, putting the rest of his books and school papers on his desk. "You don't understand, Dad. They don't treat you like this. They don't treat you like you're a walking crime, like your very existence is wrong. Like nothing you say—not the laws you know or the truth you tell—is worth anything. They treated me like a thing to be thrown around, not a person." Reed's voice is soft. He stands over his empty backpack.

"I lost it," Reed says, barely above a whisper.

"Lost what?" his dad says.

"I know I dropped my soccer ball on the train when they ripped me out of the car," Reed says, searching the pockets of his bag. He walks past his dad and back to the closet. "I must have lost the permission slip to sign up for varsity." A memory comes crashing back. "One of the cops balled it up and threw it behind the trash can. The coach said if my parents were okay with me playing with the older boys, he would let me try out. I can't make the team without that form," Reed says, becoming more frantic. "I have to find it. It has to still be there."

"What's the coach's name?" Dad asks.

"Coach Branch Rickey," Reed answers as he continues to go through his pockets.

Reed opens his closet and grabs his soccer team's hoodie. He walks out his room, and his dad follows. "Reed, what are you doing?" Dad asks.

"I need to go and get the form. I need you to sign it so I can turn it in for tomorrow," Reed says, hustling out the door.

"Reed, I don't think you need the form. We can just—"

Before he can finish, Reed rushes past his bedroom door and through the hallway. There are pictures of his parents when they were young. His dad, coming out of court in his suit and white high-top shoes. His mom when she became director, in her beautiful black dress with long, dirty blonde hair. Then picture after picture of Reed and Olive as babies.

Reed quickly walks through the hall. He puts on his hoodie.

"Hey! Take off the hoodie before you leave this house!" Dad shouts before Reed reaches the door. Reed jumps at the sound of his dad's yell, but Dad's tone is no surprise. He has few rules about what Reed can wear, but this is a big one. He can own a hoodie, but where and how he wears it is a major deal.

Reed pauses for a moment and turns around. "Or what? A cop may stop me for matching the description of someone? Oh, too late," he says, shrugging his shoulders. He turns back to the door defiantly.

Reed's words stop his dad in his tracks. "Reed!" Dad calls, this time in more of a whimper than a shout, as he tries to stop Reed from going out the door, but it's too late.

Reed halts just before he hits the sidewalk but doesn't turn around.

"Why do you think I tell you not to wear a hoodie?" Dad asks.

Reed sighs. "I think it's because other people think that bad people wear hoodies or something. I don't really know." Reed turns to face his dad. "I have friends who wear them. Even my soccer team gives them out, and people wear them to the games. I know you let me wear it at tournaments when I'm with the team, or just sitting around the house, but you don't let me wear it to go hang out with a friend down the block or when I go play in the park. But I see you wear one sometimes. So I don't know." Reed shrugs as he walks back to the front door.

"A hoodie just isn't safe for you in certain places." Dad's voice is calm now. Tired. But he walks to meet Reed halfway. "It's a combination of things, some you can control, some you cannot, some you'll grow out of, some you won't. A hoodie by itself, especially when you put it over your head, is seen as a kind of cloak, I guess. You see a person with a hoodie, and what do you think?

That the person is hiding something? That they're trying to be alone? And if you're a forty-seven-year-old Black man walking with his two kids in Brooklyn, that's a lot different from a group of Black teenagers in hoodies walking down those same streets. So you're not allowed to wear a hoodie when you're out with just your friends and especially not when you're by yourself. Maybe when you're older, maybe when officers stop seeing you as just 'matching the description,' but until then, you will never leave the house with a hoodie unless the circumstances make it safe."

Reed meets his dad at the stairs leading to their front door. His fists clenched with anger. "Yeah, I get that, Dad. But I wasn't wearing a hoodie earlier!"

Dad and Reed both stand at the front of stoop, staring at each other. "I wasn't hiding my face or looking like I was trying to avoid someone. It wasn't my name, or the way that I spoke, that they could have judged me on. I was wearing high-tops, jeans, a button-down, and a *blazer*! A blazer, Dad! How could I, a fourteen-year-old, match the description wearing those clothes?" Reed says, pleading with his dad for a response as he tugs at the clothes he's wearing.

"Not wearing a hoodie at your age is a cautious way of trying to shield you, to protect you, from the assumptions and prejudices that may affect the way you're seen in school, on the streets, and, if need be, when speaking with cops. But protection does not make you invulnerable. We try to wear this 'armor'—walking a certain way, talking a certain way, dressing a certain way—in hopes that it will protect us. We create this false sense of security that we are protected. But when we see someone like us wearing the same armor yet getting harmed or killed, it's a grim reminder that that armor we wear isn't really protection from anything."

Reed's dad stands at the front door and wipes his eyes as he clears his throat. "Me, my dad, his dad before him—we all did our best to keep our kids safe. But we can only do so much. There are no guarantees once you step out of this front door."

Reed shrugs and walks back to the sidewalk, starting down the road. His dad hurries behind him, trying to get him to stop. "Come on, don't walk or get on the subway again today. Let me give you a ride."

Reed weighs his options. Ride with dad or take the subway. He nods and follows his dad.

Dad unlocks the car doors, and after the two of them get in, they just sit there for a moment, not saying a word.

"The exact thing that happened to you has never happened to me, but I think I can still help," Dad says as he starts the car and pulls out of the parking spot. "I don't think there's a Black male alive who hasn't been harassed or abused or at the very least embarrassed because of some assumption a White person made about them. I can't count the number of times I've been at court, wearing a suit and carrying a briefcase, and have been told that I can't sit in the front row of the courtroom because it's for lawyers and police only. Your uncle got pulled over and had his car searched for drugs because a White police officer thought a Black guy driving a new BMW was 'off.' And you remember when the cashier at the 7-Eleven made your cousin empty his pockets to prove he hadn't stolen anything?"

Reed nods. He remembers it all. And these examples are making him feel worse, not better.

"The fact is, Reed, no matter how we dress or what we do, there is a chance we'll be judged and treated based on nothing but the color of our skin." Reed's dad shakes his head and laughs, but it isn't a happy sound.

"What's so funny?" Reed asks, peering up from under his hoodie.

"Nothing's funny, but sometimes you need to laugh to stop from crying. Because you're learning the dirty little secret that is impossible to know until you've experienced it yourself: you're not alone. Nearly every Black professional I know has had the exact same experience. Being told where they can and cannot exist. That they cannot be in a certain space because, to another person, they don't belong in that neighborhood, in that luxury store, or in the courtroom."

Reed feels despondent. Clearly, it doesn't matter how

good a student he is, how good of an athlete, how good of a person. He may never be safe or respected because of the color of his skin.

His dad unclenches his fist around the steering wheel and turns to him. "I've thought a lot about what I would say when or if this ever happened to you. But still, I don't have all the answers. What's the right thing to say? What have other parents said to their kids? What did my father say to me? How do I feel about cops personally, and do I want you to feel the same or come to your own conclusions?" Dad says.

"I don't know how I feel," Reed says. "I mean, I don't know how I feel about all cops. I know how I feel about those cops today!"

Dad nods. "Yeah, I don't know how I feel about them either." He puts the car into park. "The truth is, I don't know that I can just say something to make what you're feeling go away and keep this from happening again. And I know that's not what you want to hear, and it breaks my heart to tell you that. But not having the answers and not trying to help are two very different things."

"I know," Reed says. "Thanks for trying to help."

Dad pulls Reed close and hugs him.

Reed hugs his dad back. He knows they both need it. That they're in this together now. And somehow he feels better knowing he isn't alone in this.

Reed's dad pauses for a moment. "C'mon, let's go

find your permission form. And maybe you can walk me through what happened. The more I understand, the more I can help you."

"Okay," Reed says, though his stomach is tying itself in knots at the thought of returning to the scene of the worst experience of his life.

They get out of the car and walk to the train station. Reed starts to become nervous as he gets closer. His dad sees this and suggests they find a bench to sit on outside. Reed sits next to his dad with the weight of the world on his shoulders. "Okay," he says, "So this is what happened . . ."

Reed sees his dad go through a roller coaster of emotions as he explains everything.

"And I'm sorry I got arrested," Reed finishes. "I'm not that person. You and Mom raised me to not be that person."

Dad starts to tear up. "Never, ever apologize for this. This is not your fault. You did nothing wrong." He looks at Reed. "The unfortunate reality is you don't have to do anything wrong for things like this to happen. Philando Castile wasn't doing anything wrong when he legally carried a gun. Breonna Taylor wasn't doing anything wrong when the cops raided her home. Police harassment—or worse—doesn't only happen when you do something wrong. I shouldn't have to teach you how to stay safe with cops. I shouldn't have to teach an unarmed fourteen-year-old how to be safe around trained adults in body armor and guns. They should be the ones working to be better.

But the reality is, I don't have time to wait for the world to become safer for my children, so I have to have this conversation with you now. But never take on the faults and ignorance of others. That's not on you—it's on them.

"Never apologize for what those cops did to you. Do you hear me!?" Reed's dad says forcefully.

"Yes, Dad," Reed says. He has to stop himself from saying, "I'm sorry," from apologizing for apologizing.

"Reed, are you . . . are you okay?"

"I w-was . . ." Reed stammers quietly. He sniffles and rubs his eyes, trying to hold back tears. "I was just so scared when it all happened. It honestly happened so fast I didn't even know what was happening. One second, I was walking out of the train, trying to get all my stuff, and the next I was up against a wall with a bunch of cops all over me. Once I figured I was being arrested, I tried to stay still or do what they were yelling at me to do, not giving them a reason to think I was a threat, just like you told us to do. But I couldn't stop shaking. The officer kept screaming, 'Stop resisting, stop resisting.' I wasn't trying to be tense or resist; I wasn't trying to flex on him or fight him. I was just so afraid. In that moment I felt like if he took me, it would be over for me. I know that doesn't make sense as I say it now. But at the time I wasn't thinking, Oh, *they are going to bring me to a judge, and the judge will release me with a court date.* They attacked me like I was getting jumped, so my body reacted to that."

Reed takes a deep breath before he continues. "I could have sworn I wasn't coming home tonight. I didn't know what else to do but just . . . just give up, I guess. I don't really know. I just *stopped*. I can't explain it."

Reed and his dad get up from the bench. "You're safe now, don't worry. Let's go get the form and head home." Reed and his dad stop at the top of the stairs heading down to the station where Reed was stopped and handcuffed. Reed speeds down the stairs to the turnstiles, wanting to get this over with as quickly as possible.

"Let's get this form and get out of this place," Reed's dad says as he pays for them both to get onto the platform.

Reed walks through the turnstile, then turns left. He freezes for a moment, staring at the empty platform.

"Is this where it happened?" his dad asks gently.

"Yeah," Reed says, so softly he almost can't be heard. "Just over there." He points to the bench he sat on, handcuffed, not even an hour ago. "It felt like I sat there forever, until one cop told the others, 'Let him go.' Something about how they already got the kids they were looking for. They uncuffed me. Made it seem like this was all my fault. Then they left as quickly as they came. Didn't say anything about arresting me. No explanation, no apology. Nothing!" Reed's voice shakes with anger. "That's where I just gave up."

CHAPTER 9

Decide Not To Be Reduced

Maya Angelou

"BUT YOU WEREN'T 'GIVING UP' in that moment," Dad says as they continue to stand on the platform.

Reed walks over to the trash can close to where the officer had patted him down, searching around it for anything that looks like the form he lost. His dad follows, getting on his hands and knees to look under the nearby bench.

"We've talked about this. You may have experienced this for the first time, but it doesn't change what you were taught. That was not a moment of weakness but a moment of strength. You have power over yourself. You have the power to control how you react. The cops want you to react, since they understand their power increases when you react to them. Speak, and they can search.

Resist, and they can arrest. Fight back, and they can hurt you. When you channel your pride and your intellect, you harness the power you have and take their power away from them rather than giving them the power to search, arrest, or harm you. You are not a second-class citizen; you are not what they perceive you to be. You are strength. You are wisdom. You are excellence. It's not about giving in or giving up to them. It's about the power you hold. And how you can best use it in that moment."

Reed spots a balled-up piece of paper on the floor. Could it possibly be the permission form? He opens up the paper, hopeful this is it. His head sinks.

"Everything okay, Reed?" Dad asks as he places his hand on Reed's shoulder.

"This isn't it. It's not here," Reed says, disappointed.

"I think that form is lost, Reed. I'm sorry, but it is the New York City subway station. Let me see that piece of paper," Dad asks with a smile. Reed hands it over. His dad writes on the page and hands it back to Reed. Reed looks over the page and mumbles to himself. The page now has a sentence about permission to try out, the date, and his dad's signature. Reed looks up at his dad, a hint of hope returning. "Losing something and not being able to move forward are two very different things, Reed," Dad says. "And if this doesn't work, text me when you're at school and I'll come in and sign the form myself at your tryouts. Sound like a plan?" Dad flashes Reed a comforting smile.

"Thanks, Dad," Reed says, the hint of hope growing as he hugs his dad.

Reed steps back, sits on the bench, and looks over his prize with a smile.

"Hey, Dad?" Reed asks as he looks at the signed paper.

"Yes, Reed?"

"This is great and all . . . but this paper is a little dirty. Do you think you can sign another one for me when we get home?" he says with a smirk.

Dad can't help but smile. "Sure," he chuckles. They sit there for a moment, Reed remembering the last time he sat on this bench—not even a couple hours ago. His dad is right next to him. Neither says a word. Reed's smile vanishes.

"But I don't get it, Dad. I thought if I dressed like this, stayed away from trouble, and did what you told me to, I would be okay."

"What do you mean, 'dressed like this'?"

"You're always telling us to dress a certain way, to walk with our heads held high. 'Don't wear baggy pants with your underwear showing.' 'Don't wear hoodies.' 'Have this brightly colored wallet.' 'If you have your headphones in, don't turn them all the way up.' It seems like we do so much to change our everyday lives just to be safe. But what did all that do for me here? You tell us about your clients and how they are profiled by the cops and even the courts. That in certain neighborhoods cops will stop a person just because of how they look. That they will frisk them and arrest them even for petty crimes, hoping to find something more, hoping that a person reacts. But it didn't matter today, Dad. They saw me, but only what they wanted to see in me—not the person I actually am. They just saw a description, and the fact I looked close enough was all they needed to accuse me of a crime. None of this kept me safe, Dad!" Reed says, tearing up.

Dad leans over in the seat next to Reed and grabs him with both arms, holding him tight to his chest. Reed feels a pounding heartbeat, louder and harder than he's felt before. He thinks his heart is going to jump out of his chest. Then he realizes that he isn't feeling his own heartbeat. It's his dad's.

Dad holds him tight and tighter. Reed realizes his dad isn't trying to comfort him; Dad's scared himself. So Reed hugs him back, hoping it will help his dad.

"You got home safe, though. You're safe now," Dad says as if trying to assure them both. "C'mon, let's head home." His dad gets up and extends his hand to help Reed up off the bench.

Reed takes the hand and gets up.

On the drive home, Reed and Dad sit in silence, both lost in their own thoughts. Until Reed says, "You always talk about fighting back, making it so this doesn't happen to people, especially people with less who don't have a voice in this system. It's been going on for hundreds of years and hasn't stopped. What do we have to do to get this to stop? For them to stop looking at us like this? They treated me like a piece of trash they could throw around, like nothing. I'm not that person. I don't do the things they thought I did. I don't hurt people or steal. I didn't do anything wrong! I felt kind of guilty when I walked home because I knew what I experienced was just a couple of bad minutes with the cops that I got to walk away from. But what about other kids who get stopped like this and end up worse off? Kids who don't have the status and ability to fight back like we do? If it happened to me, then how many kids have those cops done this to? How many more will they do this to?"

Reed pauses for a moment and then says, "I don't know what would have happened if that officer didn't get a call that the kids who actually walked through the train had been caught. Would I be in jail right now? What would I tell my teachers? 'I missed class because I was being arraigned'?"

His dad pulls the car up in front of the house. Reed turns in his seat to head out the car, still half talking, half mumbling to himself. "What would I have told the coach when I missed the first day of tryouts? Would I have been kicked out of tryouts? School?" Reed doesn't wait for his dad's reply. He opens the car door and heads into the house, his head spinning with what could have happened.

Dad rushes to follow. "Reed—" But Reed is already inside by the time his dad catches up with him.

Reed continues to voice his spiraling thoughts. "And when the officers told the others what had happened, their story changed to make it seem like they didn't just drag me through the subway train and station for no reason. The police were lying. Why would they lie? What did they have to gain? It makes no sense. If they could lie about something like this, then what else could they lie about?" Reed is pacing in the kitchen, his eyes darting around, not focused on anything in particular.

"Hey, Reed. Reed!" His dad shouts to try and get him out of his head. Reed is jolted out of his thoughts and turns to him. "Breathe. Reed. Breathe. Trust the cops or don't trust cops. You can do whatever you want to do after this. You wouldn't be wrong either way. But cops are just people with badges. Some are safe, and some are dangerous. Six months of training, a gun, and a badge don't change who a person is. Good people make great cops, and bad people make dangerous cops. I don't think that will ever change. But we also have to understand and respect the power they have. Trust that they can protect us but also harm us. And understand the power they have over us, our lives, our liberties, and others. Make sense?"

Reed lifts his head to think for a moment and nods, agreeing with his dad. Dad continues, "Understand that we live in a world where a trained, armed, and protected cop can legally act out of fear and kill you. But you, an unarmed and untrained teenage boy, have to remain calm with a gun in your face." Dad puts his arm around Reed. "But you know what? You're home safe now, and that's all that matters. Let's get you and your sister something to eat."

Reed sits at the kitchen counter as his dad starts grabbing plates and cups.

Reed watches his dad put beef patties on a baking sheet and slide them into the oven to cook. It's strange, being in his house, watching people do everyday, normal things after what just happened to him. "You know what really hurt that I never thought would?" he says, his voice barely above a whisper. "The cops just walked away laughing. What were they laughing at? Why was this funny to them? Were they laughing because they knew they got away with this? And I know what you're going to say. 'It's not all of them,' but where were the 'good ones' when I was being jumped? I didn't see any. One officer ripped me out of a train, and they all just ganged up on me."

Reed pauses for a moment. "But, thankfully, one officer—the sergeant—asked questions and helped figure out what was going on. But she didn't stop them. She didn't stop that knee from being driven into my back. She didn't stop the handcuffs from ripping through my wrists or stop my body from being thrown to the ground. So what am I to thank her for? That I didn't get locked up for something I never did? That I didn't die? Is that how low the bar is for dealing with cops? But if it wasn't for her . . . I don't know where I'd be. I don't know what would or could have happened to me. And that scares me," Reed says. "Dad, I just want to know how to not become a hashtag."

Reed looks to the man who taught him so much. But Dad's face looks just as worried and lost as Reed feels. The man Reed has never seen at a loss for words stands stunned and silenced by what Reed is asking.

"I was innocent. I am innocent," Reed whispers to his dad.

"I know, Son. I know."

"I don't even want revenge on that one cop. I want change," Reed says.

"I know. Me too."

As much as Reed wants Dad to have the answers, it's a relief to sit in silence for a moment, both of them wanting the same thing, without excuses or explanations.

Finally, Dad breaks the silence. "Let me see your wrists."

In his anger, Reed forgot how much his wrists hurt. He looks down at them as Dad gently holds them and turns his hands back and forth. The skin on his wrists is very red; the inside of his right wrist looks like it's already starting to bruise.

"How do they feel?" Dad asks.

"The burning feeling is almost gone. They just feel

sore when I try to move them, and my shoulder feels funny. I don't know how to describe it." Reed flinches when his dad touches his shoulder.

Dad stands straighter, like he's listening for something. "Olive, I know you're listening from the hallway. Your beef patties are heated up. You can come in and grab them from the kitchen counter if you want." He pulls three carbonated grapefruit juices out of the fridge, opens them, and hands one to Reed.

Olive comes from the hallway around the corner. "Oh, hey, Dad, I was just looking for my books," she says, though Reed knows she's been eavesdropping.

"Sure, sweetheart," Dad says. "Come join us and grab some food." He points to the food and drink on the table. Then his face shifts a little. "Actually, Olive, do you have your phone on you?"

"Yes, Dad."

"Can you take pictures of your brother's wrist and shoulder? Then we'll look at the videos you took."

"Okay," she says, eager to be helpful.

Reed holds his hands out and lets Olive take a picture of them.

"You did the right thing taking all those videos today, Olive. You were right to document what happened to you and Reed. When, or if, you are asked in court about what happened, you'll be able to say how Reed got those injuries and what they looked like once you got home. Maybe there is a case against the cop. Maybe there isn't. But it won't be because we were not prepared. The info you've collected could be useful in fighting for accountability."

Olive beams. "Thanks, Dad. I did my best . . . but—"

"No buts, Olive. You did amazing. How about this: I know it was probably hard to do on a subway," Dad says as he scoops ice into a bag, "but maybe you remember things that happened that didn't make it on the video. Do you think you could go write those out for us while I finish looking after your brother?" Dad tightens the knot on the bag of ice.

"Yeah, I can do that. I already started," Olive says as she quietly sifts through her notebook.

"Here, grab this," Dad says to Reed as he tosses the bag of ice.

Reed grabs it with both hands.

"Looks like your shoulder is just sore, nothing's broken or dislocated. That's good. Use the bag of ice on your shoulder. When you're done eating, we'll go to the hospital and have it checked out."

Reed begins to eat, and with every bite, he remembers how hungry he was when he left school. "It's not that bad, Dad. I've had worse. I don't need to go to the hospital."

"I want medical records close to the time you got injured so if we do fight this in court, we have the right tools. Medical records are an impartial expert opinion saying you were injured," Dad explains, then takes a sip of his drink.

"Makes sense," Reed says, but he feels a sting of guilt. He knows that not everybody who gets injured by police can afford a trip to the hospital.

"So we're going to fight this, Dad?" Olive asks. "We're going to go to court and hold those officers accountable for what they did to Reed?" As Reed eats, his dad takes a long sip of his drink. Dad's eyes are filled with disappointment and sadness as he searches for the right response.

Their dad pauses, unable to give an answer. "I don't know. First, let's make sure everyone is okay."

Even he doesn't know the answer, Reed thinks.

Reed looks up at his dad, still chewing the massive bite he just took. He gulps. "Why don't you know, Dad?" Reed mumbles with a little food still in his mouth. He can see that his question hits Dad hard. His dad always has the answers. Dad may not be the smartest man in the world, but sometimes Reed feels like he is. Because his dad always has something smart to say about anything and everything. But this time, Reed's question is met with silence.

"I know you have a lot of questions," Dad says, "and I don't know what it will take for them to stop treating us like this. I don't know the answers to your questions because I'm still trying to figure them out myself. We all are still trying to figure them out." Reed swallows the last bit of food in his mouth. Both he and his dad sit in silence for a moment, staring at their feet, defeated by their inability to find an answer.

"Not everything that is faced can be changed; but nothing can be changed until it is faced." His dad's voice sounds far away, like he's lost in a memory.

"What?" Olive says. "That doesn't make any sense!"

"It's a quote by James Baldwin. I'm not sure yet what we're going to do about what happened to Reed today. But I know that there are pieces of this system that are broken and it isn't going to get fixed on its own. It's going to take many of us, maybe all of us, to make this better. You and Reed can learn about it, you can be vocal about what you see wrong in the system, but for now I just want you to be children, and I want to keep you as safe as possible."

Dad reaches across the table to take Reed's and Olive's hands. "For now, the only thing I need you to do, the most important thing I need you to do . . . is *come home safe.*"

PART 2

COME HOME SAFE:

From the Café

CHAPTER 1

If They Don't Give You a Seat at the Table ... Bring a Folding Chair

Shirley Chisholm

"SO, WAIT. THAT MEANS A COP doesn't have to read you your rights before they arrest you?" Olive whispers to herself in shock as she looks up from her book. She closes it, saving the page with her finger. She pauses for a moment, thinking about the words she just read and how they play out in real life.

It's early spring in Brooklyn, one of the first nice days of the year, and Olive is sitting on a bench in Fort Greene Park, reading about the law. All around her, people are working out, families are having picnics on the lawn, people are walking their dogs. But Olive sits off to the side, a little bookworm buried in a book full of highlights and tabs.

Olive nods, satisfied she understands what she just read as she opens her book to read more. "You have the right to remain silent. Anything you say can and will be used against you in a court of law. You have the right to an attorney. If you cannot afford an attorney, one will be provided for you . . ." Olive skims through the words of the Miranda warnings officers sometimes give to the people they've just arrested.

Her mind drifts off, thinking about when it would make sense to speak to the cops in an interrogation. *Why would anyone ever speak after hearing this? Wouldn't it be better to speak to the cops after speaking to a lawyer? They may not even know what they're actually being charged with when they're getting questioned.*

Olive and Reed have always loved going to Fort Greene Park on Saturday morning, especially when their mom does her weekly boot camp workout class there. But Reed doesn't really come to the park that often anymore. When he does, Olive has realized something different about Reed when he's in the park lately. He isn't as interested in playing. This morning, Mom had to push him to come out so he wouldn't spend his time kicking a ball around in his room by himself. But even with the push to come out today, Reed isn't playing soccer with everyone else like he used to. Instead, he's off to the side, still kicking the ball around all alone.

Olive picks her head up from her book as she thinks about Reed. She looks around and spots him, headphones in—most likely with the volume turned all the way up—training on the far end of the park. He has his cones and soccer balls out, the whole nine yards. Just running drills on his own, drowning out the world around him.

Last spring, Olive and Reed went to the park all the time. Sometimes they hung out together, but they also liked doing their own things. Olive would read or stroll over to the farmers' market to see what new things the vendors were selling, and Reed would play soccer with kids his age most of the time; sometimes he put up cones and helped little kids learn how to kick or dribble the ball.

But both of their attitudes have changed since his experience with the police. Olive doesn't explore the farmers' market with a big smile full of wonder and surprise like she used to. Now, Olive takes reading her law books a little more seriously. And Reed chooses more and more to be alone.

Olive turns back to her book. "So, Miranda warnings are just about getting a person's 'legal permission' to get info from them . . . so the cops can use what they say against them later? They're not even a requirement before you can get arrested," she says to herself as she writes a note in her book. She looks up into the tree, chewing on the end of her pencil. "I guess that makes sense. If you were caught on camera stealing a candy bar, the police might not say the Miranda warnings because they wouldn't have to ask you questions. They would just look at the video and arrest you. What questions would they have to ask, really?" she mutters to herself. Then she wonders, *Should Reed have talked more to the police when they stopped him? What would be the point of even speaking to them, other than for them to try and get him to incriminate himself?*

Ever since Reed was handcuffed and thrown around by those cops in the subway, Olive has been reading more and more about people getting arrested and the laws behind arrests. She remembers that when the officers pulled Reed out the train, she was paralyzed and terrified about what could happen to him. She was filled with self-doubt, thinking, *There's nothing I can do. I'm useless; I'm helpless.* And so many questions ran through her head: *Are they going to take Reed off the train to question him? Where are they going to take him? What are they going to do?*

But it wasn't just in that moment, or just that day, that the voice of self-doubt whispered in her head. This whispering continued until she finally answered back, *I'm never going to be helpless again.*

Now the questions running through her head are looking for solutions. *How do you make sure you can protect yourself and those you love so you never freeze, never feel useless, again?* The answer? *I'm going to know the laws inside and out. That way I'll never be helpless like that again. If I know the law, I can stand up for myself and the people I care about. I've just got to keep reading, keep learning.*

Reed's arrest changed Olive. For her, learning the law isn't just about being like her dad anymore or having a fun project to think about with him. Instead, it's about being prepared to protect herself, her brother, and maybe one day others, from going through what Reed experienced. She's even more motivated to become a judge.

After Reed was handcuffed, Olive filed a complaint at the precinct, but nothing has really happened since. Olive pleaded with her dad about suing the city over what they did to Reed, but they never did. Even though Olive understands why they didn't, it still bothers her deep down.

"I don't think you're going to like what I have to say," Dad explained when they made the decision. "Maybe the fact that there was nothing on Reed that would suggest he was smoking would help your argument. But . . . I don't know if that would change anything."

"What do you mean? Change what?" Olive pleaded.

"Legally, what the officers did may not be wrong." Dad shrugged off his words as he explained why the case may not be winnable. And why worst of all, Reed would have to relive the arrest over and over again. "The police would be protected by what's called qualified immunity, and what they did would probably not be considered a 'deprivation of rights' for Reed."

"What's qualified immunity?" Olive asked, worried about what that could mean for her brother. It was the first time she'd heard the phrase. That day, she found out she was right to worry.

"It's a legal policy that protects people who work for the government, like police, from being person-ally responsible for monetary damages due to violating another person's rights, like using excessive force."

Maybe I should take a break from reading for the day, Olive thinks as she lies on the bench. *Not like I'm going to change anything, right?* Olive gets off the bench. Just remembering what happened to Reed is making her agi-tated. She can't help but relive that day as she reads more about the laws the officers should have followed. *Let me just walk this off and clear my head. Maybe I'll go to the farmers' market. I haven't been there in a while.*

Olive walks through the rows of jams, breads, and artwork, in awe of all the things for sale—especially the pastries.

She tries to get lost in the market, but a bit of her keeps fixating on what she was reading. "Assault and bat-tery . . . unlawful touching. Nah, that wouldn't work. Excessive force . . . the cops slapping cuffs on him and throwing him up against the wall on the platform—that's gotta be something," she mumbles to herself as she weaves aimlessly through people in the market.

About halfway through the market, she thinks about turning back to see how Reed and her mom are doing. *It's still pretty early*, she thinks, looking at the time on her phone. *Mom's still working out, and I'm sure Reed is fine on his own. I'll keep walking around for a bit.* Olive looks up from her phone and notices she's near Axel's Apples, the fruit stand with especially delicious pastries, and decides it might be time for a snack.

Olive thinks back to something her dad told her after Reed came home that day. She was so motivated, so passionate, about doing something, anything, to fight for Reed. *Olive, I am not saying you shouldn't do something, but I have to let you know that this may not work as well as you hope. Yes, there are a lot of things you could argue: unlawful stop and search, false arrest and imprisonment, assault, battery, unreasonable force. You could even say that they intentionally caused emotional distress to Reed. You could sue the police department for hiring and keeping these officers on the force. There is no shortage of what you could argue. But winning can be extremely difficult. This road you are thinking about driving down headfirst, going after a police department, is not an easy one to travel. It's just smart to think about why you're going into battle before you start the fight.* But Olive has never been deterred by the hard path, especially if it meant helping her family.

Olive has been going back and forth about what happened to Reed, and what her dad told her, for months now. She's been trying to figure out what to do with it all: how she felt, what she could have done in the moment, and what it means for her and Reed now.

Olive pauses in the middle of the farmers' market, with the park on one side and vendors on the other. People walk around her to get where they're heading while she is lost in her thoughts. But she won't let what happened to Reed paralyze her. Instead, she'll let it fuel her to help bring about the change she wants to see.

Being helpless sucks, but I bet when you get older, it's a lot better. As Olive stands in line at Axel's Apples and considers what she needs to do, she feels a sense of confidence grow in her. Olive is the baby of the family. Everyone has always looked after her. She loves her family for that, especially her brother. But she's grown up fast and wants to be the kind of person who looks after her family too. To be like her brother, her mom, and her dad, and to help them like they have helped her all her life. And this, protecting her family by knowing the law, feels like the best way she can be there for Reed and make sure he always comes home safe.

The line inches closer to the front of the food stand, close enough that Olive can smell the apples and cinnamon from the tempting baked goods.

But the sweet smell of pastries doesn't distract her

long enough from what happened that day; it keeps replaying over and over in her head. She can't shake the lingering feelings of fear and helplessness. She felt them then, and she still feels them now. She spoke to her dad about what happened to Reed but never really talked to him about *her* feelings. How could she be a victim when she only saw what happened? Reed was the real victim. Still, she can't seem to let it all go.

The person in front of Olive orders a dozen apples, then steps to the side. "Good morning. How may I help you?" the young woman behind the stand asks Olive with a smile. Olive opens one of her books—she keeps a few dollars tucked in there—and notices a note she wrote to herself in the margins. "Be the change you want to see in the world." She remembers when she wrote that and told Mom her plan.

"I'm going to be a judge, who's fair and honest and helps young kids. I'm going to be my ancestors' wildest dream."

Her mother had smiled and told her, "Tomorrow you will change the future, but today you must prepare."

That was the same day she deleted the video of Reed being arrested. Even though she'd sent the video to her dad, she had kept it on her phone too. She found herself watching the video over and over again, reliving every terrifying second, and she didn't want that anymore. Olive remembers thinking that Reed looked like he'd lost everything. Everything about Reed had shifted since that day . . . it was like the officers took something valuable that Reed was lost without.

She remembers praying in those moments, *Please, God, bring my brother back home to me. Don't make him another hashtag in a long list of hashtags. Don't make this subway station the place where I have to lay flowers for my brother. Please, please, bring him home to us.*

Olive watched the video till she couldn't blame herself anymore. *Even if I was strong enough, even if I was fast enough, there's nothing I could have done to get them off Reed and get us home safe,* she finally decided. She felt relieved, and then she deleted the video, believing she could let it go for good.

"Miss, would you like to buy something?" the woman at the apple stand asks.

"Yes, sorry about that," she says softly as she closes her book. "Can I have an apple turnover, please?" Olive hands over her last two dollars.

Once she gets her pastry, she starts walking back to the park. *Justice Olive,* she thinks as she bites into the flakey turnover. *Just like Justice Ketanji Brown Jackson. I could be just like her, a public defender on the Supreme Court.*

Olive takes another bite of her turnover, enjoying its combination of sweetness and spice.

That's enough law for one day, she decides as she walks back into the park.

CHAPTER 2

The Highest Appreciation Is Not to Utter Words But to Live By Them

John F. Kennedy

OLIVE LOOKS AROUND TO SEE if Mom and Reed are finished with their workouts. Most of Reed's cones, and the ladder he brought for footwork practice, are packed up to one side, but he's still juggling the ball by himself on the far side of the park. Olive's mom and her workout group are taking a water break.

That turnover was great, but now I could go for a drink. She walks over to her mom to see if the class is almost done. "This is our last water break, love. We'll be done in about twenty or thirty minutes," Mom says.

"Is it okay if I grab a drink from that café over there?"

Olive asks, pointing to a café across the street. "I used my last two dollars on a pastry, sorry."

"No problem, but take your brother with you. Can you buy me a water too, please? And see if your brother wants something," her mom says as the instructor calls them back from the water break.

Olive turns around to see Reed juggling his soccer ball with his headphones on, probably lost in his music and his thoughts. Olive jogs over to him.

"Reed!" Olive shouts. He doesn't respond, but it's no surprise. He's in his own world as usual. Olive walks up to him and waves her arms above her head like she's signaling a plane to land, trying to get his attention. "Hey, Reed, want something from the café?" she yells, using her hand to pantomime drinking. Reed takes his headphones out of his ears.

"My bad. What's up?" Reed asks. "You getting something to drink?"

"Yeah. Mom gave me money to get something for all of us, but you've got to come too," Olive says, waving a twenty-dollar bill.

"Cool. Yeah, I'll come. Can you help me clean up first?" The siblings pick up the few cones on the ground and put them in his big bag, then drop off the bag next to where their mom is working out. The pair point out where they're heading, and their mom waves in acknowledgment.

Reed presses the crosswalk button. It beeps as they

wait for the light to change. A few feet away from the crosswalk, a homeless man is sitting up against a bus stop. He has a large bag and a sign that says, "Homeless VET. Please HELP." Olive pulls out her phone.

"Whoa!" Reed shouts as he puts his hand over Olive's phone. "What are you doing? You're not calling the cops on him, are you? He isn't hurting anyone. He's just asking for help!"

"No!" Olive shouts back. "You know I wouldn't do that!" Olive shows Reed her phone; it shows her search results for nearby shelters for vets. "I would never call the police on a person who just looks homeless, especially if they aren't really doing anything wrong. You know Dad's stories as well as I do. People getting caught up in the system." Olive scrolls down her screen. "Here, this is a decent one, and they have intakes on Saturday. You got a few dollars? I only have the twenty Mom gave me."

"Yeah. You going to give it to him?" Reed gives Olive three dollars out of his pocket. Olive takes out her note-pad and scribbles the shelter's address on a blank page.

"Thank you for your service, sir," she says as she tears a page from her notebook. "I also wrote on a note the address and directions to a local shelter that helps vets get back on their feet. And here's three dollars for the subway to help you out."

"Thank you, miss. Have a blessed day," the man says. He looks down at the sheet of notebook paper.

"You too, and you're welcome, sir," Olive says, walking back toward her brother.

"Guess you did your good deed for the day." Reed smiles at Olive as she returns to the crosswalk.

The siblings walk up to the café. "Hmm, this seems new. Have you seen this place before?" Reed asks, pointing at the café.

"Nope, but it looked pretty cool from the park, so I figured, why not? Plus, I just want a juice, so this place should work," Olive says, looking the shop up and down. Her gaze moves from the menu on the front window up to the name of the café. "The North Star Café."

It's a quiet little spot. Inside are one or two people working on their laptops, a couple eating breakfast, and an older man reading a newspaper and drinking a coffee by the window. At the front of the café, there are two little tables with chairs for people to eat and drink outside.

Olive and Reed walk into the shop and get in the line to order. "Hey," Reed says as he turns to Olive, "I need to use the bathroom real quick. Can you just get me a water, please?"

"Sure," Olive says, "but you might not be able to here." She points to the single bathroom door. It has an Out of Order sign.

The woman behind the register leans over the counter. "If you go next door and tell Yvonne, the owner, that Lillian at The North Star Café said you're a customer here, she will let you use hers, even though the store sign says her restroom is for customers only."

"Thanks," Reed says. "Don't leave without me, Olive. I'll be right back." He walks out the café door.

"And what can I get you?" the woman asks, turning to Olive.

"Can I have a medium grapefruit juice, please?"

The woman at the register smiles and says, "Sure, anything else?"

"Oh, and two cold waters, please." Olive checks her phone to see when her mom's class will end. Ten more minutes. A notification pops up on her phone: "Wi-Fi signal available."

"Do you have free Wi-Fi for customers?" Olive asks the woman.

"Yes, we do. The username and password are on the bottom of the receipt," the woman says.

"Thank you." Olive takes the drinks and steps out of the line. Reed isn't back from next door yet, so she sits at one of the tables outside.

The table still has a small plate and a glass of water resting at the edge. Olive doesn't mind; she isn't going to be there long. But before she's even sitting, a busboy comes rushing out to clean it.

"Don't worry about it. It's not that bad," Olive says with a smile, shrugging her shoulders. "I'll only be here for a minute anyway."

The busboy smiles back at her. "Hey, you've gotta let me do my job now. This is why they pay me the big bucks," he says jokingly as he clears the dishes and wipes the table.

"Thanks," she says.

"I see you have your drinks. Did you want something to eat too?" the busboy asks as he juggles the plate and cup in one hand and a towel in the other.

"No, I'm all set. I'm just going to use the Wi-Fi and chill for a minute. But I appreciate it." She sits, takes a sip of her drink, and signs onto the Wi-Fi. She doesn't put anything too close to the edge of the table, just in case someone passes by and swipes it. Just like her mom taught her. She places her phone facedown on her lap as she waits for her brother.

CHAPTER 3

A Wise Woman Will Not Be a Victim

Maya Angelou

MINUTES LATER, a woman frantically runs up to the café, barging through the front door, slamming it into the wall behind it. The older man who was reading and drinking a coffee by himself shrieks, and Olive almost jumps out of her seat. She looks back just in time to see the woman run up to the cashier. To Olive, the woman looks like she's not much older than a high schooler—maybe she's in university. She's White with brown hair, and she's wearing a light-pink sundress.

"Did . . . anyone . . . return . . . my phone?!" the woman yells from the middle of the café, out of breath.

"What phone?" Lillian, the woman behind the register, asks.

With a hand on her chest, the woman pauses to catch her breath. She's standing close to Lillian, but she still yells loud enough that everyone—even Olive sitting outside—can hear. "It was a smartphone with no case. I left it on the table outside maybe fifteen minutes ago. I was just here. Did someone return it? I'm worried someone stole it," she says, still trying to catch her breath between each word. "It was out here. It has everything on it. My work. My contacts. My entire life. I can't lose it." She walks to the front door and points to the table where Olive is sitting.

Lillian comes out from behind the counter and walks to the window to see what the woman is pointing at. The woman turns and stares at Olive's table.

"It's a pink smartphone with no case, but it has a big sticker on the back that says Live, Laugh—" The woman stops. She points to Olive's phone, still resting facedown on her lap. "That must be it!" she screams, throwing the door open and rushing over to Olive's table.

"It was right here!" she yells, turning back to Lillian, who comes sliding through the door, close behind the woman. The woman stands right over Olive, pointing at Olive's phone in her lap. "That's it! That's my phone!" she yells.

Olive looks at the woman, confused. Is she serious? Olive starts to put her headphones into her pocket.

"Excuse me, miss. But this is my phone, not yours," Olive says as politely as possible.

The woman walks right up to Olive, towering over her. Olive quickly slides her chair back and stands up. She grabs her phone, catching it just before it falls on the ground. Olive holds her phone in one hand as she sticks out her other hand toward the encroaching woman, palm facing forward, stopping the woman in her tracks.

She isn't going to snatch my phone from me.

"There! There it is! She has my cell phone!" the woman screams at Lillian. Olive steps back as the woman continues to push toward her. Olive takes two steps and immediately feels the café window pressing against her back. With the table to her left, a chair to her right, and the woman coming at her, she feels trapped. There's nowhere to go.

The woman yells, "She has my phone! She took my phone!" She screams over and over. "Give me my phone! Thief! Give me my phone!" Lillian rushes back inside.

Olive looks around for Reed, but he isn't back yet. No Mom or Dad to step in. And even though this adult is screaming at a twelve-year-old, no one says anything. For a brief moment, she feels alone. But she doesn't stay in that moment for long because she knows she can stand up for herself. Olive takes a confident step toward the woman.

Another person who works at the café comes running out toward the woman. The employee, a young man with wild hair who is wearing the café's apron, turns to the screaming woman and tries to calm her down. "Ma'am, please," the man says. "Please calm down. I'm the manager of The North Star Café. My name is Freddy. Tell me what happened. Maybe I can help."

The woman fights to catch her breath. "Like I was saying to the woman inside . . ."

The woman proceeds to hysterically tell Freddy what she thinks happened to her phone. Olive sees that people inside the café are noticing the scene this woman is creating. Even people across the street pause to see what's going on.

Freddy tries to get a word in over the woman's ranting. "Ma'am . . . if you'd just stop screaming for a . . . . Please stop screaming for a moment and calmly walk me through where you . . . last had the phone and how long ago so I can . . . try to help you find it."

Somehow she seems to have heard him between screams. "I came here to have a quick coffee, thinking my friend was going to meet me here. She canceled, so I figured I'd leave. I called a rideshare, paid for my coffee, then left. It wasn't until I got home that I checked my purse and realized my phone was missing. Thankfully, I only live a couple blocks away, so I ran back here as fast as I could to get my phone. When I got back, no one said they'd seen my phone. No one could help me. And now I see this girl with my phone at the exact seat I was sitting at. And she won't give me the phone or even let me check to see if it's mine. She's obviously hiding something."

"Okay . . . . Okay . . . . Okay," the manager keeps saying to let the woman know he's listening.

After the woman finishes, he turns to Olive. He looks her up and down, as if trying to figure out how to deal with her. He seems to be looking for something.

Is he looking for the phone on me? His eyes stop on her hand, and her fingers tightly clench her phone.

"Miss, can I see the phone, please?" Freddy asks. "The phone."

Those two words suck the life out of Olive. She looks at the manager, feeling disheartened and defeated. *What happened to, "Miss, what's your side of the story?" or, "Miss, did you see a phone when you got here?" or, "Miss, is that your phone?"* Olive thinks. She wants to be shocked or stunned, but she isn't at all. *Guilty till innocent,* she thinks to herself as the feeling of defeat slips away and is replaced by anger and frustration. In just a moment, the cell phone her parents bought her, with the case she made and has had for over a year now, has gone from being *her* phone to *the* phone based on the words of a complete stranger.

"The phone," Freddy repeats, hand extended. The woman stands behind the manager, proud that she is going to get "her" phone back.

Olive gets out of her thoughts and focuses on what Freddy is asking her. "There is no *the* phone," Olive says sarcastically. "There is *her* phone, and there is *my* phone. I don't know where her phone is, but this phone, the phone in *my* hand, is *my* phone. And I'm not handing it over to you."

"Miss, I'm just trying to be helpful, trying to figure out what's going on here. I can't have people screaming in the café, causing a scene," the manager says, looking from Olive to the woman and then back to Olive.

"What people?" Olive says bitterly. "She's the only one screaming here. And helpful? Helpful to who? Do you think it's helpful to accuse paying customers at your business of theft based on nothing but the word of an irrational lady? I have nothing to do with this woman or her cell phone, and you're trying to take my cell phone because this random woman is screaming at the top of her lungs? Because she is causing a scene, I have to be searched? Say that out loud again and see if it makes sense. Who else will you search if she tells you to? No one is making a scene but her."

Olive begins collecting her things off the table. "Hey, you know what? I'm out. I've paid for my drinks. I don't need to be here if this is how you treat your customers. I'm not going to be accused of something I didn't do."

"No! She isn't leaving with my phone!" the woman screams from behind the manager, her voice shrill.

Cell phone in her pocket and drinks on a tray, Olive shouts back at the woman, "Lady, the phone isn't yours! This is my phone, with my case on it. How about you try calling your phone with someone else's. Or maybe you can find your phone with a laptop or something. That would work better than harassing me."

"No! Show me the phone! Take off the case and prove you didn't steal it! It's mine! It's mine!" the woman screams as she sidesteps the manager, cutting Olive off. A few people in the café come outside to witness the scene. Freddy tries to get between Olive and the woman, but before he can, the woman lunges at Olive. Olive steps back, just missing the woman's hand as she swipes at her. Freddy turns and puts up his arm to hold the woman back.

"What's wrong with you?" Olive shouts at the woman. "I don't have your phone. Leave me alone!" The woman takes a couple steps back and begins pacing back and forth, glaring at Olive.

Freddy, still blocking the woman with his arm, looks at her and politely says, "Ma'am, I'm going to need you to stay calm, stop trying to attack this girl, and stop screaming as I try to get your phone, please." Freddy's reassurance seems to calm the woman down for now, as she stops pacing.

"Okay. Okay. But I need my phone. She can't take it. You don't understand—my whole life is on that phone," the woman says, throwing her hands up in a gesture of defeat.

"Miss," the manager says, turning back to Olive. He steps forward to get a little closer to Olive.

"Miss. Help me out here, please. I'm just trying to

settle this situation so we can all go on our way. If you took the phone, just return it, and I promise you, there will be no need to call the—"

"No need to call who?" Olive says sharply, cutting off the manager. Her voice isn't soft and calm; it's frustrated and pointed. "No need to call who? My parents? Your boss? The cops? Is that who you were thinking of calling? Why? Are you trying to intimidate me? What about me makes you think that calling the police on me for something I didn't do would make me more compliant? Is it my age? My gender? Or something else? What is it, Freddy?"

"Well . . . I mean . . . we should call because . . . because we need to," the manager stammers. He spins around, looking back at the woman. "Uh . . . uh . . . Ma'am, how about we go inside and use a laptop to try to find your phone? Or I can call your phone to see where it is. How does that sound?" Freddy asks the woman politely.

"No! That's what she wants. She wants us to go inside so she can leave and take my cell phone. She's right here—take my phone back! You're the manager, right? Take my phone, or I will!" She sounds like an impatient mom scolding a stubborn toddler.

Olive looks around her. People inside the café are pressed against the window, watching them. Some even have their cell phones out, recording. The sidewalk is getting crowded with onlookers.

This is getting serious real fast, Olive thinks. *I wish*

Reed were here. She looks around again to see if he's coming back. *He's way better at keeping his cool and working through situations than me. Plus, he could record everything that's going on. If I try, I won't be in the video, and what if she tries to grab my phone when I pull it out? Maybe if I . . .* Olive glances over at the growing crowd and sees different people with their phones out, recording. *Maybe I can ask them for their videos when they're done?* She tries to remember the details of people's appearances so she can speak with them afterward.

Olive also wonders if the café has security cameras. She wants to make sure that if something happens, she's in a well-lit area with cameras. She spots a camera but has to move a little so she'll be in its range. She takes two steps forward so she and the woman are both in front of the camera.

Olive can hear her dad's words ringing in her ears. *In court, your word is never going to be as strong as a video. If it's going to be your word against someone else's, try to make sure there's a recording of what happened. Thinking ahead in the moment is hard, but the clients who do, who record or remember who was there when they got arrested or attacked, can usually fare better when in court.* She looks around and thinks, *If I make sure we're both in front of the camera, we can use the video later to show what really happened. And maybe they can even find out where her phone is.*

Beyond the café window, Olive sees the busboy and Lillian. "Ask them!" Olive shouts to Freddy as he's trying to negotiate with the woman. "When I came in to buy my drinks, the cashier saw me with my phone when I asked about the Wi-Fi password. And when I got to the table, your busboy cleared it right away. There was no phone on the table when I got here. This is my cell phone. I can't believe I have to stand here and explain myself to you two! This is crazy!" Olive shouts, feeling frustrated and cornered. "They saw me come in and sit at this table. How could I have taken her cell phone, changed the password, and put my own case on it in that short amount of time with all these people around when I got here?" Olive hopes that someone will connect the dots, but her words seem to carry no weight. No matter how right she is, no one cares to listen.

The woman screams even more. "No! Show me! Take the case off! It's my phone! I can't let her leave with it. You can't let her leave!" the woman pleads with the manager.

The manager stammers, "Ma'am, I can't—"

But the woman cuts him off. "No, I'm not letting her walk away," she says as she sidesteps the manager and lunges at Olive.

This time the manager isn't quick enough to get in her way. The woman comes right at Olive like she's going to tackle Olive to the ground. Olive tries to step out of her reach, but she's stopped as her back hits the storefront wall behind her. Olive turns and closes her eyes, bracing herself for the woman to hit her. But the hit never comes. Instead, what feels like a strong breeze brushes past her. She opens her eyes, and Reed is standing firmly in front of her, between Olive and the woman.

"Hey! Hey! Hey! What are you doing to my sister?" Reed shouts, blocking the woman from his sister with his hands up. "Why are you attacking my sister?" The anger in his voice builds with every word.

CHAPTER 4

I'm Sick and Tired of Being Sick and Tired

Fannie Lou Hamer

THE WOMAN SHRINKS from Reed as his voice booms. He doesn't sound like the soft-spoken boy Olive knows him to be. Instead, he sounds like their dad.

Reed steps back, closer to Olive. She can hear him speaking under his breath to himself. "Control your anger, don't let it control you."

The words are a familiar mantra to Olive. She's heard her dad teach Reed over and over to never be controlled by his anger. To think before he acts.

"You're not going to touch my sister, so back off," Reed says, holding one arm out to keep the woman back as he uses his other to slide Olive behind him.

Olive can see he's worried about what will happen if he puts his hands on the woman, even accidentally. *What if she runs at Reed and then says he hit her because his hand is out? It would be our word against hers, and that's not safe.*

But the woman stops in her tracks and steps back from Reed. Olive stands on her toes, swaying back and forth, trying to peer over Reed's shoulder as he stands there, shielding her. Reed is tall for his age but still a baby-faced fourteen-year-old, with only a few whiskers on his chin. But right now he looks like a guard protecting Olive.

"She stole my phone! I'm just trying to take it back. Get out of my way!" the woman screams at Reed as she waves her finger in his face. "I want my phone back. Make her give it to me!"

Confused, Reed turns his head slightly to Olive. She lifts her phone to show him what the woman is talking about.

"Yeah, that's my phone. She won't give it back," the woman pleads with Reed.

Reed knows this is my phone. He's seen my case hundreds of times, Olive thinks as she sees him smirk at the sight of her phone. Olive smiles too, knowing exactly what he's thinking about her phone case.

"I don't know why more people don't know Viola Desmond," she remembers telling Reed when she took a five-dollar case and painted Viola Desmond's name and the year of her arrest on the back. "She was this amazing Canadian civil rights activist, businesswoman, and Black

Nova Scotian descent. In the mid-1940s, she was arrested for challenging racial segregation at a movie theater when she refused to leave a Whites-only area. Her fight helped start the modern civil rights movement in Canada."

Reed rolls his eyes as he turns back to the woman. From the look on his face, Olive knows Reed remembers the lecture Olive gave him when he first asked about the case.

Reed looks to the woman. "Ma'am, I know that phone case very, very well. It's one hundred percent my sister's. But if you've lost your phone, we're happy to try to help you find it. Where was the last place you remember having it?"

"We aren't helping her with nothing," Olive says, grabbing Reed's arm. "We're out. Let's go."

The woman glares at the manager. "Get my phone! She has my phone!"

The siblings turn to walk back to the park, back to their mom. But the woman circles around the manager and cuts off Olive and Reed, blocking them from leaving.

She won't let us go, Olive thinks in a panic.

Clearly startled by how this woman ran after the siblings, the manager speaks out.

"Ma'am, did you see her take your phone? Have you tried using an app to find your phone? Or, like I said, maybe I can call it?" Freddy keeps making suggestions to the woman in an attempt to calm things down.

The more he speaks, the more the woman looks at him with disgust.

Another person that works at the café walks out of the café and approaches the woman.

Reed turns to Olive as the waiter tries to calmly speak to the woman. "Olive, are you okay? I'm so sorry. There was a line in the bathroom, then this woman needed the room to change her baby, so I let her go ahead of me. I didn't think— Never mind. Let's get out of here," Reed says, grabbing the two waters while Olive backs toward the park. "We don't need to be here for this nonsense." Olive can't get a word in. All she sees is a worried Reed. In the background, she can still hear the woman screaming at them. Reed turns to start walking away with Olive, always making sure to stand between her and the screaming woman.

The woman seems less interested in fighting with Olive now that Reed is standing there. Olive begins to tell Reed what happened. "She came out of nowhere accusing me of . . ." Behind Reed, Olive can see the woman getting more and more frustrated as she speaks with the waiter.

"No! I'm not going to let them get away with my phone!" the woman says again.

Reed's back is to the woman, but Olive sees her coming. "Reed!" Olive screams.

The woman tries to reach for Olive, but with Reed still between them, she crashes into him first. The woman reaches over Reed's shoulder to grab the phone, and as she does, Reed turns his head. One of the rings on the woman's hand cuts Reed's cheek. Reed and the woman fall to the ground, knocking Olive down too. The woman lands right on top of Reed. Their drinks go flying, and the grapefruit juice Olive was holding spills all over her shirt.

Still on top of Reed, the woman scrambles to get to Olive. She claws at Olive as she screams, "Give me my phone, thief! Give me my phone!" Olive slaps the woman's hands away as Reed tries to slide out from under the woman. He tries to cover himself while rolling away from her, but as he does—

"Ahh!" Reed screams in pain. All of the woman's scratching and clawing caught him on the same cheek she cut before, opening the wound even more. As Reed and the woman start to get up and her hand hovers near his face, he pushes her away.

"Reed!" Olive screams. Blood is trickling down Reed's face. "Your cheek! She cut your cheek!" Olive leaps to her feet as she tries to get past Reed and to the woman. "That's it, I'm done being nice. No one hurts my brother and gets away—" But she's stopped. Something is holding her back. She looks to see Reed squeezing her arm tight, refusing to let go. She tries to pull her arm away, but Reed's grip gets tighter and tighter.

She pulls again, even harder than before. "Let me go, Reed. Let me go!" Olive screams.

"Control your anger. Otherwise, other people will control it for you," Reed says, sounding just like their dad again.

"What?!" Olive shouts back at him.

"Control your—"

"No. I heard what you said," Olive says pulling out her phone. "I don't know what you're talking about. No one is controlling me. But I am angry. Angry at her! Look at your face. Can't you at least feel what she did to you? Look!" Olive holds up the camera to Reed's face so he can see the cut on his cheek. "See, see what she did to you? She can't get away with that," Olive screams, still trying to pull away from Reed.

"Stop. If you let her get you so angry, you'll do something you regret. She is controlling you. She is getting the best of you. Don't let her. People sometimes don't see the first strike, but they always see the person who retaliates. All eyes, all fault, will be on you. So control your anger, or others will control it for you . . . I know. It sounds a lot better when Dad says it, but you know I'm right," Reed says.

Olive's breath is coming heavy, but she stops struggling. "Okay, okay. You're right." She keeps her eyes on the woman as she steps back, watching to see if she'll attack again. Reed turns and sees the woman is still on the ground.

"I didn't realize how hard I pushed you," he says. "I didn't mean it. When you cut me, I just reacted."

Reed hurries toward the woman and offers his hand to help her up.

"I'm so, so sorry. I didn't mean . . . it was just . . . I don't know. I'm sorry. Let me . . . let me help you," Reed stammers, trying to help the woman to her feet.

"Assault!" she screams. "He assaulted me! You are all witnesses. You saw him assault me!" Reed jumps back and covers his ears.

The woman keeps screaming. Accusing Reed of attacking her. But no one in the gathered crowd moves to help her. Her shrill voices pierces his ears.

"No! No! No! No! No!" Reed says as he backs away.

Worried, the siblings look around. No one reacts. The people in the crowd all just stand there.

"What do I do? What would Dad tell me to do? How do I de-escalate this? How do I get us home safe?" Olive can just make out Reed whispering to himself. "Stay where you are. Make sure that when the police arrive, there's nothing in your hands, no cell phone, no wallet, nothing. Make sure your ID and anything the officer may ask you for is accessible so you don't have to reach anywhere close to your waist. No sudden movements. Only move when a cops ask you to, and if you do, explain your movements." Reed talks through his dad's lessons.

The woman sits there on the ground screaming, "Assault! Assault!" over and over again. Olive spins Reed around to face her. He stops muttering to himself. She can see the worry in his eyes as the wheels keep spinning in his head.

"Don't worry, we all saw what happened," Olive says, trying to hide her fear and reassure Reed. "You didn't assault anyone. And even if cops try to say it was assault, everyone here saw what happened." Olive takes a napkin from the table and gives it to Reed, who presses it to his bleeding cheek.

"We got this."

"Thanks, Sis."

CHAPTER 5

No One Can Degrade My Soul Within

Frederick Douglass

"THIS IS GETTING OUT OF HAND," Olive says, watching the screaming woman and the growing crowd. "Maybe we should go get Mom and come back. This doesn't feel safe with just the two of us."

The woman yells to the group in front of the café, "Someone give me a phone so I can call the cops and tell them what they did to me! I'm going to tell them that an *African American* girl stole my phone and that an *African American* man threatened my life and assaulted me. Why is no one recording them? Didn't you see what this *thug* did to me?" She emphasizes *thug* as if she wants to say another word but can't or won't.

A few kids turn their phones toward her to record

the outburst. Some people chuckle and point. One voice breaks through the buzz and says, "Relax, Café Karen!" People break out in laughter. The name-calling only makes the woman angrier and yell louder.

Reed turns to Olive. "What if she does call the police? What then?"

"Then she makes a report," Olive says, keeping her voice low. "Worst-case scenario, the cops put a warrant out for our arrest, maybe a detective comes by the house, then maybe you get arrested at the house or you have to turn yourself in. If she tells them the story that I stole her phone and you assaulted her to stop her from getting the phone, that isn't a minor crime. That's a felony. That's robbery for both of us." Olive watches the woman walk right up to the manager of the café and demand that he call 911 because she had been the victim of a crime.

"Maybe we shouldn't leave then," Reed says. "Maybe we should call Mom and get her to come help us."

"Yeah. Do that. You call Mom and tell her we need her here," Olive says.

Reed calls but gets no answer. "She must still have her phone in her bag," he says. "Her class just ended . . . I'll text her." Reed speaks the message as he texts, "Across the street at the café. Woman attacked us trying to take Olive's phone. Can't leave. Come quick!"

"I guess we could run to her. She isn't that far from us," Olive suggests.

"You want a Black boy to run to the park after a White woman was shoved to the ground and is screaming at the top of her lungs that he assaulted her and his sister robbed her? Or that you're leaving with 'her' phone?" Reed says, making air quotes around the word *her*. "That's not a smart move."

"You're right. Not smart. If she calls the cops, they will say that us running shows we are guilty. Not that we are terrified of what could happen if the cops get here and believe her story instead of the truth," Olive says, her frustration growing.

Just as Olive is trying to come up with a plan, an NYPD car stops across the street from the café. The woman—who had been going from person to person, looking for someone who will lend her a phone—turns to the siblings and shouts, "Oh look, they're already here. No need to call them." She runs over to the officers as they step out of their cars. "Officers! Officers! Stop! Help!" she screams.

What happens when the cops get over here? What's going to happen to Reed? What if he gets arrested again, jumped by a gang of cops, and thrown against the wall? Olive starts to relive the day in the subway. She feels frozen in time.

"That *African American* man threatened and assaulted me after I tried to get my phone back from that girl!" she screams, hands flailing in the air as she stops the two officers at their car. Olive can't hear every word the woman is saying. But she hears *threatened, assaulted,* and *phone* over and over again.

The woman must be telling the officers to have Reed arrested and to have them take and search my phone. Olive's mind frantically goes to the worst that could happen. Sure, they'll search her phone and realize that the woman was wrong, but they still may arrest Reed and just let the courts figure that part out. He could get handcuffed again. Put in a holding cell for hours. Then maybe, just maybe, after a day, he'll see a judge and get released. All of this could happen—all of this would be allowed—because this woman tried to attack her and take her phone. Olive can feel her heart racing, and her palms begin to sweat.

Maybe she should give the police the phone. Or try to talk to them. *Am I negotiating from a position of power, like Dad always tells us?* Olive wonders. She sees one of the officers point in their direction and start to walk over to them. And in that moment, as Olive sees a fearful Reed, she knows the best way to protect him.

"I know. I'll call 911," Olive says firmly.

"What! Why?" Reed says.

"Look," Olive says, "the cops here may not listen to us because they've already got her side of the story. But if I call 911, at least the police will have the truth on record in case this goes bad. I'm not thinking about now;

I'm thinking about later." She picks up her phone and punches 9–1—and then she stops.

Only call the police if it's an emergency. Dad's words ring in Olive's ears again before she presses the final number. *Understand that once you call the police, they will do what they are trained to do. Investigate a crime. Arrest a suspect. And, depending on the situation, kill whoever they see as a danger to themselves or others. Before you call the police, understand that the outcomes of that call could go beyond what you want. Make sure you are calling the police for the right reason. Because the police are a huge and sometimes dangerous force to call on someone. Calling them isn't like calling the manager at a store. You are calling a deadly force to fix something or protect you or others. Make sure what you are calling them for really requires the police.*

Olive remembers that when he told her this, she asked, "But how would I know the difference?"

Dad said, "It's completely a personal decision. No one can tell you when you should or shouldn't call the police—that's about your level of safety at the time you call. But you should only call if you believe the situation needs a person with a gun, if a serious crime has happened, or if your safety or the safety of those around you depends on the police. But these are guidelines, things for you to think about to decide whether or not to call. Cops aren't the store manager, but they also help keep us safe. It's all about calling them when they are needed, not whenever you want."

Having already dialed 9–1, Olive says, "I understand what I am doing. I need the police here. This situation needs the police." She presses the final 1 and tells Reed, "We need to make sure that the truth, and our side of the story, is recorded by the police."

Before Reed can respond, a voice on the other end of Olive's phone asks, "Nine-one-one, what's your emergency?"

"Morning. My name is Olive. My brother was assaulted by a woman near Fort Greene Park. She scratched him on the face as she was trying to steal my phone," Olive explains.

She wants to give as much information as she can, knowing that the cops usually take the first report they receive and run with it for assaults like this. There is no big investigation. This isn't a murder case or a TV show. The cops aren't going to interview everyone at the café. They may not even check the video. They will arrest first and figure it out in court later.

Olive remembers her dad's words: *Once a prosecutor has a story of who the victim is, it's hard to change anyone's mind. But if you can show them evidence, especially when they are first trying to figure out what happened, it's a lot easier to help someone who got arrested.*

Olive may be speaking to the 911 operator, but she

is thinking about the judge, the prosecutor, and even the jury the whole time. She is focused on the "W5H" that Dad uses when he's building a case in court: Who. What. Where. When. Why. How.

"Where are you?" the operator asks.

"My brother and I are at a café by Fort Greene Park. The North Star Café."

"Do you know the cross section?" the operator asks.

"DeKalb and South Oxford, southeast corner of Fort Greene Park," Olive responds quickly, knowing that the more specific she can be, the better.

"That's in Brooklyn, right?"

The operator continues down his list of questions, asking what happened.

"Is the woman still there?" he asks after Olive gives her report.

"Yes, she is. She is screaming in the street that she got assaulted. My brother and I are still here at the café."

The operator pauses for a moment before asking, "Are you injured?"

"I'm not, but my brother is. The woman cut him on the face when she tackled us both to the ground trying to take my phone. I don't know how it happened, but when he got up afterward, his face was bleeding. He is a fourteen-year-old boy in a navy-blue tracksuit with white indoor soccer shoes. About five feet, nine inches, with a fade on the side and small Afro on top, and a cut on his left cheek." Olive wants to make sure that when the officers arrive, they know the only Black male in the situation is the victim and not a threat.

"All right, miss, help is on the way. I just have a few more questions, but don't worry, these questions are not delaying the police. I just need more information to help them when they get there. Is the woman Black, White, Hispanic, or Asian?"

"White."

"How old is she? Approximately how tall? What is she wearing? Any weapons? Does anyone need an ambulance?"

Olive answers the operator's questions one after another. "Oh, please tell the officers that I'm wearing a black top with a picture of a Black woman on it and blue jeans. I am not the White woman on the street wearing a pink summer dress. Please send help—she seems out of control."

"Okay, miss, a police officer should be there shortly."

CHAPTER 6

You Think Your Pain and Heartbreak Are Unprecedented . . . Then You Read

James Baldwin

"THE POLICE ARE ON THEIR WAY." Olive says to Reed. "In the meantime, why don't you start recording? Let's not wait till we know what kind of police interaction this is going to be. If things go well, then we can delete the video. But if it's negative, then we have a full video of what happened. We don't want people to say, 'Well, we don't know what happened before,' if something goes wrong and it becomes our word against the officers'."

Reed nods and holds up his phone, pressing Record.

"Hello, miss, can we have a word with you, please?"

Olive looks up to see an officer walking onto the curb toward them. The woman is still screaming, waving her hands in the air as she speaks to another officer, who is struggling to keep up.

"What's your name?" the officer asks softly.

Does she just stay quiet? Ask for a lawyer? Hope her mom gets Reed's message in time and rushes over? Olive runs through all of her options. "Ask for a lawyer and don't talk to cops without us," Olive remembers her parents telling her. *What do I do? What do I do? Wait for Mom, ask for a lawyer and say nothing else, or do something different altogether?* She keeps coming back to the same three choices.

She glances over at Reed. He's filming her conversation with the cop, fear and worry etched in his face. She doesn't want him to speak up. *They'll treat a teenage boy in a tracksuit harsher than they would treat a little girl,* Olive thinks. *If I stay quiet, who here will speak up if they believe the woman and nothing else? Who here will stand up for Reed? Am I not my brother's keeper?*

"Olive. My name is Olive, sir," she responds. "And this is my brother, Reed," Olive adds, pointing at Reed and his camera. The officer looks at Reed; the cut on his cheek still looks raw.

"Well, Olive, it's nice to meet you. My name is Officer Rob Smalls. I'm sure you saw, but this woman waved us down and told us you stole her cell phone from this table over here. Do you know anything about that?" The officer stands tall in front of Olive, looking her up and down as if he's searching for something. Olive pauses a moment. *He didn't even ask about Reed,* she thinks. *This cop rolled up and saw one person screaming, uninjured, and another with a visible wound. And he doesn't even ask about how the person got hurt?*

"I know nothing about her phone. My brother and I came in to order drinks. I sat down to have a drink while my brother used the bathroom next door. Then she came screaming at me, demanding that she have my cell phone because she said I—"

"When did you get to the café?" the officer says, interrupting.

"Excuse me?" Olive asks.

"When did you get to the café?" the officer repeats.

"I don't know the exact time, maybe ten minutes ago now?" Olive responds.

"Did you see a phone when you got here?"

Wait. Olive plays the officer's question back in her head. *Is he trying to interrogate me? Like I took the phone? Does he think I'm a thief?* As her mind races through what is going on, her eyes catch sight of a little black box fixed to the officer's chest. She realizes something.

"Your light isn't on," Olive says.

"What do you mean, my light isn't on?" the officer asks.

Olive remembers her dad's office door. It's always closed when he's watching camera footage or listening to 911 calls. She always wants to see what's happening in those videos, but Dad says "it's confidential" or "you're too young." He's told her about body-worn cameras and how important video of any kind is to his job. Dad explained that in New York City, and many cities around the country, officers wear body cameras. These cameras are meant to show what happens between officers and everyday people. Because for far too long, when someone was arrested, it was their word against the cops' . . . The unfortunate reality is not all cops tell the truth, because they are human. "Technology, smart phones, and the affordable portable cameras in the hands of people who are over-policed is bringing their experiences in front of millions, regardless of where or who they are," Dad had said. "These aren't just stories of officers abusing their power, planting drugs, and committing murder that have been told in communities for decades anymore. Now, there are videos the world can see. The deaths of people like Eric Garner, George Floyd, and Ahmaud Arbery became cases that changed a lot because of video of their final moments."

"I'm sorry, Officer, but my dad always says that if I'm talking to a police officer and I don't see their camera on, I should politely ask them to turn it on. You have a body-worn camera on your vest, and the light is not on. That means it isn't recording, right?" Olive says, pointing at the camera on his chest.

"Is this something you feel needs to be recorded? I'm just trying to help out here." The officer chuckles, not seeming to take her request seriously.

When Olive doesn't respond, the officer presses a button on the camera, and a light turns on. "Miss, you are now being recorded," he says, sighing theatrically.

"Good," Olive replies. "Now, I am happy to talk about how this woman assaulted my brother and tried to steal my phone, thinking it was hers."

The officer takes a deep breath, clearly annoyed by the situation. "So, the woman's phone. Have you seen it?" the officer asks.

"No, sir."

"Why are you here by yourself? Where did you come from?" the officer asks as he looks around.

"I'm not here by myself. I'm here with my brother," Olive says, looking back and pointing at Reed. "We came from the park, where our mom is."

The officer pauses for a moment, as if he's run out of questions to ask. But then he switches gears.

"And whose phone is that? Do you have proof that it's yours?" His voice sounds more serious and accusatory, but Olive's parents have taught her what to do in this situation. *Never rush to answer an officer's questions. Think about what they are asking, and if you are going to*

*answer the question, only answer that question and noth-
ing else. No explanations. Cops are trained, as a part of
their job, to see crime everywhere. And when interrogating
someone, they will see criminality in whatever you say.
It's why answering questions generally doesn't work and
why you should always ask for a lawyer and your parents.
But if answering questions may be helpful, which is very
rare, you should think carefully about what you're doing.
Because when you think you are explaining your innocence,
they could be thinking you are lying to get out of being
arrested.*

Olive thinks, *What kind of foolishness is he asking
me?* as she looks at the officer.

Instead of fighting back, she decides to play along,
being mindful of her answers. "Yes, the phone is mine.
Unfortunately, I don't walk with proof that I paid for my
cell phone. How would I prove to you that the phone is
mine? By unlocking it? By showing you that I've got a picture of me and my family on it? Here." Olive takes a step
back. She slowly turns her hand over so the officer can see
that she only has a phone in her hand. "Officer, this is my
cell phone. I'm going to unlock it to show you it's mine."

The officer squints to look at the screen, even though
he is standing close to her. "I'm sorry, I can't see the screen
that well. Can I hold the phone, please?" he asks politely,
reaching for the phone.

"No, Officer, I do not consent to you taking, holding,

or looking through my phone." She locks the phone and pulls it back to her chest.

"Keep your hands where they can see them, and don't make sudden movements," she whispers to herself. "Empty and visible. Keep your hands empty and visible." Keeping her arms to her sides seems safe in this situation because the officer can clearly see her hands. She lowers them from her chest.

She hopes the officer can also see that she does not have a weapon on her. There's nothing hidden on her or sticking out of her pants, and her hands have always been visible. Olive wants to be sure that nothing about her says "threat" or "I'm going to run." Her small, all-black backpack that says, "Nah. —Rosa Parks, 1955" is still sitting on the table outside of the café. Olive makes sure to stand far enough away from it to show that it is out of reach. But she's also made sure she's standing closer to it than the officer so he doesn't think he can search it without asking. She struggles to find a balance between "I am not a threat to you, nothing in my bag can hurt you" and "I'm not walking away from my bag so you can search it." Like everything else she's doing, the balance is about protecting herself and protecting her rights.

"You know I could just arrest you and search your phone, right? This could go a lot easier if you'd just give me the phone, and we can settle this here and now. The other way, the harder way, is that we settle this at the precinct," the officer says sternly, standing firm as he reaches out for Olive's phone. Olive looks over at Reed and sees him watching. He and Olive have been taught the same lessons, but she knows she probably paid better attention to them.

Olive knows what her mom would say if she were here right now. "It's just a phone. There's nothing on it that would get you in trouble. And they may just go on their way once they realize the woman is wrong." But at the same time, Olive is annoyed. Why should she have to give up her phone? Why should she have to give up her things, her privacy, to someone? *Why should I fear what happens to me if I don't give in?*

Here and now, Olive decides to use her power to stand up for herself. She isn't saying anything that could get her arrested, and there is no danger to her safety from the police or the hysterical woman. She knows how to handle herself. When she looks back at Reed, he gives her a nod as if to say, "You got this." Olive knows that if he thought she needed him, he would jump up and say something. His silence, and that smile, is all the support she needs.

Olive feels a sudden burst of confidence, like she does when a debate-team opponent screws up and gives her an opening. "Sir, this feels like I am being accused of a crime by an officer. If I am, I need my parents here because I am underage, and I would like a lawyer. If I am not being accused of a crime, I would like to leave. Am I free to leave?" Olive asks.

"We're just having a conversation," the officer replies.

"That didn't answer my question, so I'm going to grab my bag and go—if that's okay with you, Officer." Olive moves slowly, explaining what she is doing as she does it. She reaches for her bag.

"Stop!" the officer shouts. One hand reaches out to Olive while the other moves to his holstered gun.

Olive quickly pulls her hand back and puts her hands up. "Officer, I see that you reached for your gun," Olive narrates, knowing the body camera can't see it but wanting it to be known. "I only reached for my bag because I thought I was free to go," she continues. "Your reaction tells me I am not able to leave, that you are detaining me," she says in a loud, clear voice so the officer's body camera will be able to hear.

"No, no, it's all good," he says like he's trying to make light of the moment. But his hand is still close to his gun. "How about you take a step or two away from the bag and we try to figure out what happened to this woman's phone? Sound good?"

"Where is your supervisor?" Olive asks. "Have you called them yet?"

"Are you asking for a supervisor or are you asking if we called one?" the officer asks sarcastically. Olive steps away from her bag, and the officer moves his hand from his holster.

"I asked, 'Have you called them yet?' because as a

MOS, when you have a report of a stolen phone, you're supposed to call your supervisor after you've interviewed the victim." This is another technique Dad taught her about being questioned by the police. *When you're talking to cops, using their language—like MOS, or Member of Service—makes them stand up a little straighter and respect you a little more. It's like letting them know, 'I know what rules we're supposed to play by, so you can't cheat me.' It sucks. They should just show that respect to everyone, but unfortunately, that's not where we are yet.* Olive wants this Member of Service to understand that she knows the rules he is supposed to follow.

The officer raises his eyebrows, seeming part skeptical and part impressed. "My partner is going to call our supervisor when he's done speaking to the woman whose phone was stolen," he says. "Now I'd like you to let me look at your phone. You can give it to me, or I can arrest you and take it from you."

Olive's palms begin to sweat. She imagines what she wants to say to the officer. "You're absolutely right, Officer. You probably could arrest and search me. Searches after a lawful arrest are very much allowed in New York. But are you sure this is a lawful arrest? What crime would you be arresting me for? Or are you going to arrest me and then try to figure it out later? If so, that's not allowed. So go ahead—arrest me, a twelve-year-old girl, for allegedly stealing a phone when you have no evidence other than this woman's words. But then you would have to explain to your supervisor, the prosecutor, and most likely a judge what your reason for arresting me was. Or maybe you could actually investigate the case while you're here instead of going to what's easiest and trying to forcibly take a phone from a kid. Will you speak to the cashier who saw me come in with this exact phone and ask for the Wi-Fi password? Will you ask the busboy who cleared the table before I sat down? Or, even better, will you check the video surveillance that's in the café? I don't know. But before you arrest me, does it seem to be more probable than not that a crime has actually happened here and that I am the one who did that crime, or does it seem like this woman lost her phone and is blaming the first person she can? It seems you're just thinking of arresting me because she told you to, and that's not the way this works."

That's what Olive *wants* to say to the officer. It's what she's dying to say to the officer pressuring her to give up her phone. It all plays out in Olive's head as if she were a lawyer in court arguing her case. She wishes she could say every word to the officer just as she imagined. But would her words change anything? Would the officer magically agree with her and just let her go? She knows he wouldn't. She has very little power here. Here, on the street, she is powerless trying to negotiate with a police officer. And it terrifies her. In the streets, like her dad tells her all the time, she is negotiating from a place of weakness.

Olive stands there, phone in hand, trying to figure out what to do next. She's scared about what could happen to her and her brother, what the officer will do if she does or doesn't give up her phone. "It comes down to trust versus fear," she remembers Dad explaining. "When the police stop or question or even try to arrest you, it's scary. It's scary because you don't know what *they* are capable of. You're giving yourself up to a person who has a lot of power over you, a person who knows there would be very few, if any, repercussions if they harmed you. When I was young, I felt terrified when the police stopped me or questioned me. But after I went to law school and then became an attorney, I understood how to advocate for myself and others, and more about what the police could and couldn't do to me—and my fear shifted to trust in myself. I knew I could survive each encounter to fight elsewhere. You have to try your best to not act out of fear. And if you can't trust that the officers will keep you safe in their custody, trust that I will get you home safe no matter where you are. But you've got to stay safe so I can get you home safe, Olive."

This isn't the right place to fight this battle. She considers everything she's learned about what police are allowed to do—and what they're not allowed to do. She thinks about all she could say, all she wants to say, but shouldn't. Lost in her thoughts, Olive stares at her phone.

"Give me your phone, miss," the officer insists, more forcefully this time.

A phone is an object you purchase, Olive thinks. *It's totally replaceable. You can't replace your brother's life or your life. Things are never as important as your safety, as your dignity, as your family.*

It's just a phone.

"Officer, you know what? Here you go," Olive says as she lifts her phone to the officer.

CHAPTER 7

In a Rage Almost All the Time

James Baldwin

BEFORE OLIVE CAN HAND OVER the phone, Reed is suddenly beside her. He slowly steps in front of her. She looks at him and sees a big smile. Reed looks up at the officer. "Um, Officer. Before we do anything else, call supervisors or whatever, can we call our parents? I'm only fourteen, and my sister is only twelve. I don't think we should continue until we have our parents here. Especially our dad, who is also our lawyer. He is a homicide defense lawyer here in Brooklyn."

The officer looks shocked. His eyes dart from Olive to Reed like he's trying to figure out his next move now that he knows their dad is a lawyer. "Um, just . . . just stay here for a minute. Don't go anywhere," the officer stammers as he turns toward his partner and the woman.

"Ma'am, can you stay right here?" he says to the woman, who is standing with the other officer.

"Officer Colvin, can you step over here for a minute, please?" Officer Smalls says, signaling the officer to join him. They step back from Olive and Reed while clearly watching them. A few moments later, they walk back over to the siblings.

"Okay, kid, let's try it your way and call your mom's number." Reed narrates his steps of pulling up the phone app and dialing.

"Car four sixteen, are you in the vicinity of DeKalb and South Oxford, the southeast corner of Fort Greene Park?" the radio on the officer's shoulder screeches. "We have a ten-twenty-four, past assault. Suspect is a White female in her early twenties, five feet, five inches, wearing a light-pink dress. The victim is a twelve-year-old girl wearing blue jeans and a black shirt with a graphic on it. She is in the area in front of The North Star Café. Please respond if you're in the area." Officer Smalls leans his head closer to the radio on his shoulder to listen.

He looks Olive up and down, scanning her clothes. He turns to look at the woman speaking to his partner, then looks back to Olive.

For the first time in this conversation, Olive feels hope. Maybe calling 911 really did help. Maybe the officer will now believe what she's been trying to tell him this whole time. Officer Smalls radios back that he and his partner are there. "Did you call nine-one-one on this woman after she accused you of stealing her phone?" Officer Smalls asks.

"No," Olive says sharply, "I called nine-one-one after the woman violently tried to snatch my phone from me and cut my brother's face with her nails or something sharp when she tackled us to the ground. Then she screamed and yelled that an African American man assaulted her, trying to escalate the situation, and put us in danger . . . that's when I called nine-one-one, sir," Olive says, correcting the officer as she stands just a little taller.

Officer Smalls hesitates, looking like he's not sure what to do next.

"Stay here," he tells Olive. The officer walks over to his partner, who has already gone back to speaking with the woman after hearing the call. All three walk over to Olive and Reed.

"That's him, Officer. The man that assaulted me," the woman says, thrusting her finger toward Reed. She hides behind the officers as they walk toward Olive and Reed, as if she's afraid of the siblings and needs to use the officers as a shield.

"She stole my phone, and he assaulted me when I tried to take it back," the woman says.

The officers approach Olive. The officer who has been talking to the woman walks right up to Olive. She looks at the front of his uniform, trying to read and remember her name. "C. Colvin," she reads off his badge.

"Miss, can you give the woman her phone back? If you do, we can just resolve this here. We'll call it a mistake, and we can just be on our way."

"Officer, I don't have her phone. I never had her phone. My brother and I have no idea what she is talking about or where her phone is," Olive says, standing closer to Reed. Olive brings her phone up from her side, and slowly, she presses in her password. "See, Officers, it's my phone," Olive says. "It's the phone I came to the café with when I walked up and bought my grapefruit juice. It's the phone I pulled out when I asked Lillian for the Wi-Fi password. It's the phone I used when I called nine-one-one, telling the operator that this woman assaulted my brother by scratching his face and also tried to steal my phone. I'm not going to give you my phone in this moment because I shouldn't have to. We are the victims here, not her," Olive says, arm still extended with her palm facing the officers. Out of the corner of her eye, she catches a glimpse of Reed. He's once again recording it all.

Suddenly, a loud "Hey!" cuts through the group. The officers, the woman, Olive, and Reed all look in the direction of the scream. It's Olive and Reed's mom, running across the street from the park, with her bag and Reed's slung on her back. "What are you doing to my children?!" she screams at the officers.

Olive watches the officers look at their mom, then

look back at her and Reed, as if it takes them an extra moment to connect that a White woman could possibly be their mother. Officer Colvin's demeanor also shifts as he suddenly becomes polite. "I'm sorry, ma'am, are you these children's . . ."

But before he can finish, a car honks loudly behind them. On the road, just behind the officers and the woman, a cab driver is standing in the doorway of his cab. In his hand, raised above his head, he holds a cell phone. The driver waves the phone, yelling, "Ma'am, you forgot your cell phone in my car! Ma'am!" he keeps shouting, trying to get the woman's attention.

One by one, the officers, Olive, Reed, and people watching turn to the cab. The woman looks to the cab driver, then to Olive. Her head slowly drops, and her face turns red with embarrassment. A look of shame washes over her as she and everyone around begin to understand what Olive and Reed have known all along.

"Ma'am!" the cab driver yells again, trying to get the woman's attention. She quietly turns around and shuffles to the car, grabbing her phone.

Officer Smalls walks up behind her. "Is that your phone, ma'am?" he asks.

"Yes, I think so," she says softly. "Now that I have my phone, I think I'll go home now," she says confidently, making every attempt to avoid eye contact with the siblings. There's not a single tear in her eyes now, as if the last half hour never happened. The trembling and hysteria in her voice have vanished.

"Um. Excuse me! Why is my son's face cut?" Olive's mom interjects. Officer Smalls walks back to Olive's mom, both hands facing her as if to calm her down.

"Ma'am, it appears this was just one big misunderstanding. This woman mistakenly thought your daughter took her phone. There was some shouting, we came in to try and figure out what was what. But it seems like the mystery is solved, and we can all go home," Officer Smalls says with a smile, as if he has accomplished something.

"Go home? I'm asking you how my son got cut, and you're telling me everything is fine and that we can just go home? What is wrong with you?" Olive's mom snaps back.

"That woman scratched him trying to take my phone from me," Olive says.

"She did this! Are you going to do something about it?" Olive's mom stares down the officer.

He shrinks under her words and turns to the woman. She is scrolling through her phone.

The officers both walk toward the woman. "Ma'am, let's have a talk down at the station." Officer Smalls takes her phone out of her hand and gives it to Officer Colvin, then he grabs her by the wrist and places her arms behind her back.

"Wait, what? What's going on? What are you doing? Where are you taking me? I thought she stole my phone, that was . . ." Her voice fades as the officers put her in the back of their car and close the door behind her.

Mom turns toward Reed and Olive, giving them both a huge hug. "Are you two okay? I ran over the second I saw your text. I was so scared when I saw those police coming toward you, Olive. Reed, are you okay? Let me see your face."

"We're okay, Mom," Reed says, smiling and taking her hand off his cheek. "It's just a scratch. I've had worse, you know that." The cut on his cheek is no longer bleeding.

"Olive, are you okay?" her mom asks, checking her for injuries.

"I'm fine, Mom," Olive says, but she doesn't feel fine at all.

"Ma'am," a voice behind their mom says politely. She turns to face the officer. "Would you like to file a police report?" Officer Colvin says, holding on to a piece of paper and a pen.

They all stay for a few minutes as their mom has the officers listen to Olive's and Reed's description of the events.

"I think we're done here," the officer says as he finishes his report. "I'd expect a call from the district attorney's office asking if you want to press charges."

"Thank you," their mom says.

The officer walks back to his police car, his partner and the woman still waiting inside.

Proudly, their mom turns back to Reed and Olive.

"Let's take a cab home instead of walking," she says, pulling out her phone to order a ride home.

CHAPTER 8

What You Endure Does Not Testify to Your Inferiority but to Their Inhumanity

James Baldwin

"TELL ME HONESTLY, are you two okay?" Mom asks as soon as they are all in the cab.

"Mom, it's not that bad, don't worry. I'll just put a Band-Aid on it when I get home. Maybe it will make me look tough," Reed says with a slight smile, trying to reassure his mom.

"And what about you, Olive?" her mom says.

"I'm not hurt, Mom. It's just . . ." Olive stops midsentence. She crosses her arms and turns to stare out the window. "Me a thief!" she mumbles under her breath.

"All based on some woman's stupid, crazy, ignorant word. It made no sense. Me! I stole her phone, put on a different case, and sat there at the exact same place she left her phone? Ridiculous," Olive continues to mumble to herself, still looking out the window.

Reed and their mom can obviously hear her mumbling to herself, but they let her vent as they ride home.

The cab stops at their house. Olive continues, "The worst part? They didn't arrest her because of what she did to us. They only arrested her because my mom, an adult and another White woman, told the officers to arrest her."

"Olive!" her mom calls out as Olive throws open the cab door and rushes up to their house. "Olive!"

But Olive is already pushing the door open as she steps inside. She heads straight to her room and slams the door. As she sits down at her desk, she starts digging through the stack of books and papers. "Where is it? Where is it! I know it's somewhere around here," Olive mumbles to herself. She pulls out a large book from the stack and slaps it on the desk. She throws it open and begins furiously flipping through the pages.

"Olive, is it okay if I come in?" Mom asks, gently knocking on the door.

"Sure," Olive responds without looking up.

Olive's mom probably recognizes the book she's reading because of its ruffled edges and the many tabs that

Olive has put in it. It's one of the law books she's been reading lately.

"I'm fine, Mom," Olive says quickly, eyes still glued to her book.

"You know it's okay not to be fine after what just happened, right?" her mom asks as she slowly walks over to Olive. She puts her hand on Olive's shoulder.

Olive turns around with a slight smile. "I know, Mom. I'm okay—I promise. I'm just looking for something." Her focus returns to the text in front of her. "I thought it would be in this book . . . . Got it!" Olive exclaims as she points to a paragraph she'd highlighted. Her mom comes from behind her and stands at her side to see what she's pointing at:

People v. William II

Reasonable suspicion represents that quantum of knowledge sufficient to induce an ordinarily pru- dent and cautious person under the circumstances to believe criminal activity is at hand.

Quantum—definition: a required or allowed amount

"I knew they didn't have reasonable suspicion. They shouldn't have been able to search or arrest me. Regardless of what she told them, they didn't have the right to search me. It's a sliding scale; you can't just take what one person says and run with it. Everything they learned, everything they saw, should have told them they couldn't search me," Olive says. She points to another highlighted paragraph. "This could be an answer too."

> When the police effectuate a seizure—rather than an arrest—based on

Her mom moves her hand from the page.

"How about we put the book away for now and just talk?" Mom says. "Even if that's what the police are supposed to do, that doesn't mean it's what they could do.

"I can't tell you what to say to the cops or what law gives you what right. But I know how to keep my daughter safe. The reality is, your dad and I don't have the luxury of teaching you what to do based on what the police *should* do. We have to teach you to watch for what they *could* do. Because this is an actual reality for you, even if it may not be for others. Remember when you were younger, and we taught you dog safety? You used to think that just because you had a big Doberman, all big dogs were safe. It's the same thing. I know that not every dog will bite you, but I had to teach you to watch for the ones that may. When it comes to some police officers, we can hope they will follow their training, but I have to make sure you are ready for what could happen if they don't," Olive's mom says.

"Now, I want to know: How are you after all of this?" Mom asks gently.

Olive closes her book. "You want to know how I feel? I'm pissed. I'm angry. I'm scared. I'm disappointed. I'm worried. But what's that going to do? Sitting here in my feelings doesn't fix anything." Olive picks up her book and stands. "I'm just trying to . . . I don't know. Obviously, knowing the law and your rights means nothing when you're out in the real world. It's whatever the cop wants to do, right? Someone accuses you of a crime. The cops assume it must be true! Even if it makes no sense! So what's the point of any of this, really?" she says as she throws her book across the room.

The room goes silent for a moment. The only noise is the sound of Olive's heavy breathing.

Then her mom gets up and walks to the book, looking less mad than heartbroken. She bends down and picks it up. As she walks back over to Olive, she fixes a few of the tabs.

"I know this is very different from what you're going through, but I think I kind of understand. I can appreciate hoping for change, hoping that the world will be fair and just, and seeing that it isn't always like it's supposed to be," Olive's mom says, holding the book as she fixes the bent pages. "I remember protesting every day for Proposition 209 in California. In the nineties we thought we were the next generation of the civil rights movement." Her mom's eyes shine with hope. "Even before you were born, we protested. My parents—your grandparents—were hippies, and we were so optimistic. We thought that we were going to be the ones to achieve equality. The hopes and dreams of Martin Luther King Jr. would come true on our watch. So we spoke up. We shouted. We screamed for equality. But now, it's different. We never thought that thirty years later, the world would be so much worse, so much more dangerous.

"But I was just naive. Maybe I didn't see the ugly side of how Black and Brown people were being treated in their communities. But I see it now, and its realer than ever," she says with sadness and doubt in her voice.

Olive turns to her mom and says, "I wasn't there, so I don't know if it's gotten better or worse. But I can tell you this: the police don't care about me or women who look like me. Women of color. Breonna Taylor, Sandra Bland, Natasha Mckenna, and Michelle Cusseaux were all killed by the police. But the problem isn't just police killings—it's killings in general with no justice. Riah Milton and Dominique 'Rem'mie' Fells were Black trans women who were brutally killed. We're targets for violence, and justice is usually beyond our reach."

Olive picks up a small stack of papers she printed. "Look," she says as she hands Mom article after article about the different women who didn't find justice. "But you wouldn't understand," Olive says, her eyes beginning to water. "Once you got there, it was all 'Yes, ma'am. Will do, ma'am,'" she says, puffing out her chest and imitating the officers. "The cops did everything you told them to without even questioning it. But me—I was invisible. I was unheard. I didn't matter."

Olive's mom pauses for a moment. "You're right. I don't understand. I may never understand what it's like for a woman, or a girl, of color to go through what you went through with the police today. But I'm here. I'm willing to listen and help however I can." She sits on Olive's bed, placing Olive's book on her lap. She opens the book and scans the pages. "Can you tell me more? About what happened to you today and what this means?" her mom asks softly, pointing to a line in Olive's book.

Olive paces back and forth as she tells her mom the details she's left out before.

"Why didn't you call me?" Olive's mom says, anger rising in her voice. "Why didn't you just give the woman your phone? It's a phone! We could buy a new one. Nothing in this world is worth that. Not getting hurt, arrested, nothing. There are so many ways this could have gone badly for you and your brother, and over what—a phone? You don't know that woman's intentions. You don't know what she could have done to you and Reed."

"Yeah, I know, Mom," Olive says. "But I did think it through. I pushed as hard as I thought I could. Made sure I was polite and didn't push things to a point where

Reed or I was in any danger. But if I was fully White, would you tell me the same thing? Or is that something you'd tell me no matter what I looked like? And if you wouldn't, why should I be less so I can be safe? How is that right? Why should I give so much? I walk differently to be safe, I speak differently to be safe, I dress differently to be safe. How much of myself do I have to give up to be safe? Sometimes, enough is enough, so why hand over my cell phone just because a woman was aggressive with me? Where does that end for me? Who do I become if that's what I do?"

Without waiting for an answer, Olive continues to explain how the police got there, how she tried to tell them what really happened, and how they didn't believe her. "Oh, and I also called nine-one-one to file a report," Olive adds, almost forgetting she did that.

"Why did you call the police? Why didn't you just hand over your phone?" her mom asks again, trying to understand.

Olive pauses and thinks for a moment. "I needed a report to be filed. The police were already there, and I thought they were coming to arrest Reed or maybe even arrest both of us. So I thought that if we were going to be arrested, I needed to make sure there was something, anything, on the record that told the truth. If I didn't, and we were arrested, when I told the truth people would have said, 'Oh, you're just accusing that woman to get back at her.' Whenever a woman is a victim, everyone always wants to talk about what she should have or could have done after the fact. And I didn't want that. I didn't want to be the victim. I wanted to be in control of my body and my property."

"I understand and respect that. But sometimes you have to make difficult choices. And your safety is always more important than your property. Which is why you should've handed over the phone!"

"Maybe. Maybe that would have been the easy thing to do. But, again, why should I have had to do that? Her story was so crazy. So ridiculous that it makes me wonder: What were the officers' intentions? What were they really trying to do? There's no way they could have actually believed her. It's like Officer Smalls was so lazy he couldn't be bothered to think about how impossible the accusation was.

"I'm tired of this lack of training garbage that people keep arguing," Olive says forcefully. "'They need more training *this* and they have a difficult job *that*.' What training can you give these two officers to help them learn common sense? What training can you give to make them hear us or see us? Nothing that woman said made sense. Nothing. But I was the criminal. I was the one that was wrong in their minds. Why? Because she said so? What about what I said? Why did her words matter more than mine? Were they truer than mine? What's the difference between me and her?

"If the choice is between a Black girl and a White woman, I know who cops, a manager, the world will choose. Some things never change. I guess having my voice heard isn't a privilege I'm allowed to have," Olive says, drying her eyes.

"Hmph." Olive's mom makes a slight noise under her breath. "I never thought I'd see the day," she says as she gets up and looks around Olive's room.

"What day?" Olive asks. She has no idea what her mom is talking about.

Her mom, still not looking at Olive, walks along the outside of the bedroom, looking at the different posters and pictures hanging on the walls. She pauses at a picture. "Who is this?"

Olive doesn't know why her mom is asking questions she already knows the answers to. Maybe the stress of the day has been too much for her? Olive looks at the picture. "Marsha P. Johnson."

"And what did she do again," Olive's mom asks like a teacher leading a class.

Olive realizes what she's doing but answers anyway. "She was a Black trans woman. Many people believe she threw the first brick in the Stonewall riots, pushing back on police brutality in New York City against people in the LGBTQIA community in the sixties," Olive says, straightening up.

"Okay," Olive's mom says. She takes two more steps

and stops in front of a poster of a younger girl walking toward a school, surrounded by protesters.

"And who's this?" her mom asks again.

Olive is still wiping away her tears, but she answers, "That's Ruby Bridges. At six years old, she was the first person to desegregate an all-White school in Louisiana in the sixties."

"Interesting," Olive's mom says like she's hearing this for the first time. "And what about this woman?" she asks, quickly stepping across the room to a small picture on Olive's desk. Olive smiles a little. "That's Madam C. J. Walker. She was one of the first ever self-made American millionaires."

"Hmm, interesting," Olive's mom says as she pretends to scratch her head.

"I know what you're doing, Mom."

"Me? What am I doing?" she says, hiding her smile.

"You want to tell me that I shouldn't give up. That so many women who came before me faced hard times and kept pushing forward. For themselves, for the world, and for me. That things are hard, will be hard, will get hard, but that is not a reason to quit." Olive grins. "Thank you, Mom." Olive gives her mom a hug.

"You surround yourself with so many strong women, you idolize them, not realizing your own strength. I saw that strength today, and I see it every day. But I'm your mother, and I worry about you. I want to make sure you're safe."

"I know, Mom, I know," Olive says. "My job isn't to fix the world. For now, my job is to make sure I come home safe."

Mom cups Olive's face in her hands. "I know that strength will guide you in the right direction. This reminds me of when you first met Judge Walker in Brooklyn, remember that?" Olive's mom sits back on the edge of the bed. "He was the judge in the young adult courtroom who Dad said you should meet when you first decided you wanted to be a judge. Do you remember how he told you about the time he was pulled over by the police? How he felt, and how it's happened to him even as a judge?"

"Yeah, I remember."

"And what did you tell me you learned after speaking with him?"

Olive sees what her mom is trying to show her. "I get it, Mom."

Olive's mom smiles. "Get what?"

"It wasn't just that he was profiled by the police when he was young and driving in a car. The point of his story was how he's used his experiences to help him be a better judge. He's compassionate but tough and has learned to balance justice with mercy. It comes from his experiences. He turns the bad into something good. He didn't let a negative experience, that feeling of helplessness, hold him down. He actually went out there and became a judge to give hope to the hopeless," Olive says.

"You are far more than what other people treat you as—never forget that. Quit or don't quit. Fight or don't fight. Be the woman who changes the world for other women. Those are all options. But you will never give up because of what someone else does to you. You are not that person—we did not raise that person—and you are so much more than that," Olive's mom says.

Olive walks over to her desk and grabs a tissue to dry her eyes. Then she extends her hand to ask for her book back. Her mom hands it to her.

"You know what, Olive? You're right. Maybe it's because I'm a White woman. I didn't have these conversations with my parents when I was your age. And some of your cousins won't either. So maybe if you weren't half Black, I wouldn't tell you this. But what I'm doing, I believe, is keeping you safe based on how the world may perceive you and the dangers that come with that. I would say it's like how warnings people give young men differ from what young women are told because the world presents different dangers for you both."

"'We are protecting you from the world as it is, not as we hope it to be,'" Olive says, quoting her parents. "But for how long?" she asks. "Till I'm eighteen and an adult? Till I'm thirty and working a career, grown, and living on my own? And do I just say the same to my children and their children? What if Martin Luther King told MLK Jr. to accept the world as it is? Or what if Rosa Parks or

Fredrick Douglass believed that's what they should do? Would you have been able to marry Dad today? Would he be a citizen? Would I be alive?" Olive asks, confidently pushing back on what her mom said.

"No," her mom says without an expression. "Most of those things would not have happened if those people got the same advice I am giving you. But those people aren't my twelve-year-old daughter, and I am not willing to send my daughter out there to right the wrongs of the world if there is even a one percent chance it means I won't get to see you walk through that door safely." Her voice trembles a little.

Olive pauses to think about what her mom just said.

"I get that," she finally replies, the confidence and frustration in her voice moments ago slowly drifting away to be replaced by the unsteadiness of self-doubt and worry. "But this isn't just about fighting for others. It's also about fighting for myself. I wasn't standing up for myself because I was thinking of other young Black girls. I was thinking of my safety and Reed's. I felt like I was screaming underwater. And no matter what I screamed or how loud I screamed, the officers couldn't hear me," Olive says.

"Do you know what it's like to know the law, understand the law, and still have people treat you like less than?" she asks. "You and Dad raised me to be strong and to speak up when I see something is wrong. All the women in my family—my grandmas, my aunts, you—you're all so strong. But I felt so weak," Olive says, slowly closing her eyes. The confidence flees her voice. "With those officers and that woman, how they accused me, how they treated me . . . I felt less than. Like I was less than a person. Like I was less than who you and Dad raised me to be. Even though I'm home and safe with you now, I can't shake that feeling for some reason. It feels like it's gotten under my skin, and nothing will get it out." When Olive opens her eyes, she can no longer hold back the tears.

Her mom leaps from the bed and hugs her. She squeezes Olive tight as she says, "I never want you to feel like you are less than who you are—not in this house and not when you walk out these doors. Never.

"I think today, you learned that not everything can be explained in your books. That knowing the law and how things play out in real life, especially in the heat of the moment with an officer, can be very different. I understand the desire to fight and push back, but too much is at stake for a twelve-year-old, especially my twelve-year-old. I'm sorry I did not pick up my phone soon enough, but you showed you had the strength to stand up for yourself and also look for help. I want you to keep that strength. God knows you have plenty of it. But I also want you to grow in wisdom."

"Honestly, I am so glad that you got there when you

did because they would have just let that woman go. And what if the cab driver hadn't come back? She would have gone on accusing, threatening, and assaulting us, and what would the cops have done? 'It was just a misunderstanding,'" Olive says, mocking the officer. "But it sucked because it felt like her words and your words carried more weight than my words ever could. Like my voice didn't matter. Like no matter how right I was, no matter how much I knew about the law or police procedures, I just had to shut my mouth and give in to whatever everyone else said. Will that change when I get older? Or does the color of my skin dictate how much weight my words will hold for the rest of my life?"

"Maybe, maybe not," her mom answers. "But the question at your age isn't what the world will say or what the cops will do. The question you should ask yourself is: How do I get home safe? Whatever is going on in the world is going on. I'm in the here and now trying to keep my children safe in a sometimes-unsafe world. When I heard a cop was questioning you, I was terrified. I would rather your rights be violated, your cell phone get taken away, than have someone take you away from me," her mom says with a quaver of fear in her voice.

She places her arms around Olive and gives her a big hug. She gently kisses Olive on the top of her head. "You are a lot more like your dad than you know, Olive. Fight. Fight with all your heart to make the world a better place."

She squeezes Olive tighter and tighter. "With your voice, your passion, and that sharp mind of yours. Don't let anyone take that from you. And as you go out there and fight for yourself and others, just make sure—no matter how you use that sharp tongue and that even sharper mind—that you always *come home safe.*"

EPILOGUE

"*HEY, REED. WON'T BE ABLE* to pick you and Olive up from school, stuck at work. Do you mind getting yourself and Olive home? Sorry." Reed reads a text from his dad.

School ends in fifteen minutes, so Reed texts his sister. "Hey, Olive, looks like we are walking home tonight. I'll pick you up from school."

It's a hot and humid mid-June afternoon as the Elijah McCoy High School students are let out. Reed rushes to Olive's school. The weather forecast calls for heavy rain within the hour, and he wants to get home before it pours.

"Hey, Olive," Reed texts. "I'm outside the front doors. We're walking home; Dad can't make it. Looks like it's going to rain soon. Hurry up."

Ten minutes later, Olive walks out of her school.

She walks down the school steps with a group of friends, stuffing her books in her bag. Reed waits somewhat anxiously at the bottom of the steps, in front of the main entrance.

"Reed, over here," Olive calls frantically when she spots Reed.

"Slow down, Sis, it's okay. We don't have to race out of here," Reed says with a giant smile.

Olive puts her last book in her bag and zips it up. "So what happened with Dad?" she asks.

"He said he was stuck at work and asked me to get you home," Reed says as he turns to walk down the stairs. "Come on, let's go."

As the siblings walk home, dark clouds begin to pass overhead with thunder crashing in the distance. "Hey, Reed," Olive says. "What if—and hear me out because we aren't that far—we just took the four train home? We're only a few stops away."

Reed looks nervously at the sky. "We can make it home. Don't worry. Let's just walk a little faster. C'mon."

Reed sees Olive stop for a second and shake her head as his fast walk turns to a slow jog. *C'mon. We can make it. We don't have to take the train.* And then he feels it: the biggest single drop of rain ever hits him straight on top of his head. It stops him in his tracks, and he looks up. All at once, it starts to pour.

Reed pulls his backpack over his head. He has no umbrella; he didn't think he would need one today. *What do we do?* he thinks as he huddles under his bag.

Olive sprints right past him. Without thinking, he follows her. At the first light, she makes a quick right.

"Olive, where are you going?" Reed calls. "We have to keep going straight to get home!"

Then he sees the familiar green metal of an underground subway entrance. Now he understands why Olive turned right.

"Olive!" Reed shouts. But she's already at the bottom of the stairs. Reed freezes at the top of the stairs. This is the quickest and easiest way home, and he knows it. But it means riding the same train line as before, something he hasn't done since he was handcuffed by the police.

"Reed, the train is going to be here soon. C'mon," Reed hears the faint voice of his sister echo from below. "I've already put money on a card for us, and I've swiped already. C'mon!" Another echo climbs up the stairs.

"Ugh!" Reed grunts, knowing it would be silly to miss this train, especially if Olive has already paid. With a deep sigh, he slowly walks down the stairs.

"Oh good, you made it. I'm just refilling a MetroCard for us. Mine didn't have enough money when I tried the first time," Olive says.

"But you said you already swiped in! That's why I came down," Reed cries, frustrated as he looks up to see when the next train is coming. "Ten minutes." He turns back to Olive, even more frustrated. "And the train isn't going to be here in just a couple of minutes!"

Olive takes her MetroCard and turns to Reed with a confused face. "First of all, I said I already swiped—I didn't say that I was in. Second, I said soon, and time is subjective. Considering I had to refill a new card and I didn't know how long it would take for you to get down here, ten minutes felt soon to me. But, hey, look! You're here, you're out of the rain, and we are twenty minutes away from getting home. You're welcome," Olive says with a smile.

"You're welcome? *You're welcome?*" he says in disbelief. "You know I don't—I mean, I haven't taken this train in a while now. Why would you trick me into taking it?" Reed demands.

"Reed, it's raining cats and dogs out there. We are heading home, and we were half a block from the subway station. I'm not tricking you. I made a smart decision, and probably the right decision too. In a couple of weeks, the school year will be done, and you haven't taken this train once since that day." Olive hands Reed the MetroCard. "Don't you think it's time to change that?"

"It's not that easy," Reed says, looking at the MetroCard in Olive's extended hand. "I can't . . . I can't just . . ." Reed stammers, trying to find the words. "Here, give me a second. I can order us a cab."

"No, Reed. We're taking the train. By the time the cab gets here, we'll already be on the train, and we are only a few stops from home," Olive says in a soft but firm voice. "It's time. I've watched you avoid this train for months. We've walked home in the dead of winter. You've ridden your bike when it's a hundred degrees outside. You're running out of allowance money buying cabs to get to and from school when you can just take the train," Olive says, tears welling up in her eyes. "I know why you do it, even though we don't talk about it—none of us do because we know how difficult it is. But don't you think it's time? I'm here. Let's do it together." Olive takes Reed's hand and places the MetroCard in it.

Reed looks down and spins the card in his hand. "It's time? What about you? Don't you think *it's time* too?" Reed says in a mocking voice.

"What do you mean?" Olive says, sounding shocked.

"You may not have stopped taking a subway line, but you put that giant black sticker on your case that says 'Property of Olive' with your picture and Dad's office address on it," Reed says, pointing at Olive's phone in her hand. "What happened to the Viola Desmond case that you made by hand? I know it's been covered up for months now too. Ever since that woman said you stole her phone. You've changed too!" Reed says.

Olive looks at the giant sticker on her cell phone.

She slowly starts to scratch off a corner of the sticker with her fingernail. Little by little, she lifts the sticker until she can pinch the lifted corner with two fingers. Then with one quick move, she rips it off. She marches past Reed with a determined look and slams the balled-up sticker in the trash, then she marches past Reed again with the same determined look. She walks up to the turnstile, swipes her card, pushes to the other side, and turns around. Reaching over the turnstile with the card, she looks at Reed and says, "What's your excuse now?"

Reed looks up at the train schedule. *Our train is two minutes away.* His gaze shifts back to Olive, who's standing on the other side of the turnstile. He knows there's nothing he can say now to change her mind. He turns back to the stairs. Rainwater is rushing down them like rapids on a river. It's raining even harder than when they got into the station. He looks down at his phone. The app is still trying to connect with a driver, and it says there will be extra surcharges because so many people are ordering rides at once. He knows how hard it is to find a cab in Brooklyn when it's raining like this.

Reed looks up at Olive again. They can both hear the train coming. But Olive says nothing; she just stands there waiting for Reed to decide his next move. With a deep sigh, he walks over to the turnstile and swipes himself in just as the train is pulling up.

Olive jumps up and down with a big smile as Reed walks through the turnstile. "I knew you could do it!" she screams. She gives him a big hug. "I knew you just needed a little push," she says, holding him tightly. But Reed isn't as excited.

The train doors open, and Olive squeezes past the crowed to get on. Reed takes his time, sliding in once everyone has gotten off and everyone who needs to get on the train has gotten on.

He steps on the train and just stands there, looking up and down the train car, thinking of what to do next. Olive sits in a seat right next to the sliding door, in the middle of the train. As the doors close behind him, a voice comes over the speakers: "Next stop, Franklin Avenue/Medgar Evers College." Reed jumps a little as the doors slam. He stands with his back to the closed door, next to Olive. He looks up and down the train, watching everyone and everything, including the doors at the end of the train car.

The train speeds down the track, but to Reed, it feels like forever before they get to the next stop. He whips his head back and forth and turns toward every sound he hears on the train.

Olive reaches over and grabs his fist as it clenches his pant leg. "It's going to be okay, Reed. We're going to be okay," Olive whispers. The side door of the train opens up, and both siblings' heads whip over to see who is there. Reed's grip on Olive's hand tightens, and his palms begin to sweat.

"Showtime!" one boy screams as he and two other boys come through with a Bluetooth speaker playing music. Reed's grip on Olive's hand tightens at the loud scream, then relaxes.

"Don't worry, Reed. You're okay. Nothing bad is going to happen," Olive whispers, squeezing his hand. But Reed doesn't say anything. He slides his hand out of Olive's and keeps watching the doors at the ends of the train car. "This is Atlantic Avenue, Barclays Center terminal," a voice over the speakers says as the train pulls into the station.

Reed steps to the side of the door to let people on and off the train. The doors close behind him. "Next stop, Nevins Street." He puts his back to the door and watches the ends of the train again, still as jumpy as before. The train bumps and rattles from the Nevins Street station, and the doors open. "This is Nevins—"

Before the voice even finishes announcing the stop, Reed is sprinting past the turnstile. Olive chases after him.

Reed stops just before the top of the stairs, still in the subway station and out of the rain, when she catches up to him.

"I'm not like you, Olive," Reed says without turning around. "I can't just move on. I can't just put a sticker on it and pretend it never happened. It's not that easy. Every time I even think of the four train, about that day. Then I think, *What if?* Because as bad as it was, it could have been worse. Like, what if the sergeant didn't come and slow things down, figuring out right from wrong? What if she was a lazy officer and just said, 'Whatever, let the courts figure it out'? What if they never caught the kids before me—or never reported that they did? What would have happened to us then?" Reed says, looking at Olive. He's filled with terror not only for himself but also for his little sister.

"What would I say to our parents if you got hurt or you got arrested because of something that I did?" Reed asks. "That's why I don't go on that train anymore—because I don't want to have to think about it anymore."

Olive stands in front of him, a few steps lower on the stairs. She pauses for a moment. Reed stands and waits, feeling exhausted and frustrated.

"For the record, I don't pretend it never happened," Olive says softly. She moves to the side of the stairs and leans against the rail as if to get comfortable. "Pretending it never happened, and letting it get to you to the point where you stop taking the train home from a place you go to five days a week, are two very different things. A lot of things could have happened. But they didn't, and living your life based on what-ifs only hurts you and those of us who love you. Every day, Mom, Dad, and I see you prepare and change your whole schedule just so you can take the bus for an hour instead of taking the train for fifteen. We can see how this is wearing on you, and we just want to help. I—I just want my brother back. And I thought if I got you to take the train, then . . . I don't know."

Reed sees how much this means to Olive. He steps down and leans his shoulder on the wall next to her. "Well, I did take the subway. You made that happen . . . with the help of a little rain," he says with a smirk. "And maybe—maybe you're right. Maybe this has been going on for too long," Reed says, looking down at the subway.

He feels proud of what he did but still a little scared. "I guess at the end of the day, closing yourself off to your loved ones isn't the answer. Leaning on one another when times are hard is," Reed said somberly.

The siblings stand there for a moment, smiling because Olive helped get Reed here. And as Reed smiles and laughs, he feels a weight lift off his shoulders. He turns and realizes it has stopped raining, and the sun is coming out. "Hey," Reed says between giggles, "you ready to head home now?"

AUTHOR'S NOTE

MY JOURNEY IN WRITING THIS BOOK started with my wife, who initially motivated me to take on this challenge. "Why write a legal book for lawyers? Why not for kids?" she said maybe four or five years ago now. I'd jokingly brought up the idea of authoring a book about jury selection for lawyers. Her idea was better, but I didn't do much with it for months, maybe over a year. She'd said it should be a book for kids, and so my first thought was, *Well what about for our kids? How would I teach them about their rights?* At first, I imagined a collection of stories that would teach a few basic lessons about how to "properly" and safely know and invoke your rights. I had the idea of two sibling bears interacting with a park ranger and invoking their rights. I worked on the story from time to time, and I saw it as a fun project that I would use when I was eventually blessed with children.

During the summer of 2020, the world saw the deaths of numerous people of color at the hands of the police. This in and of itself was not necessarily new, but because of body camera and cell phone videos, and perhaps because we were all quarantined due to the COVID-19 pandemic and more focused on the news and social media than usual, we saw the moments that led up to the police interactions and these people's horrible deaths.

As a public defender and television host/legal analyst, I was fully aware of these cases. I'd covered many of them and even sat in the courtrooms for some as well. So it was no surprise when I got a call from my younger brother, who wanted more information about the deaths of these people who looked like him.

To understand this call, you have to understand the relationship I have with my brother. My parents divorced when I was really young, and my mother had a son, my brother Tyler, who is twelve years younger than I am. My brother and I lived together until I moved out for college. When he was born, I was one of the first to hold him. I potty trained him, taught him how to shave, bought him his first suit when he graduated from high school, was there for him after his first major breakup . . . you get the picture. When I was eighteen, I asked to become his legal guardian, and when I was twenty-one, I got a tattoo on my left wrist that says, "I Am My Brother's Keeper." So when my brother called me, it wasn't just one brother asking the opinion of another brother. Our history is thick, and I have a responsibility to him as more than just a brother.

Tyler asked, "How do I not become the next hashtag?" Even in the context of the conversation, I was confused and taken aback. We were talking about Elijah McClain and how he died. How he did nothing illegal and was basically jumped by the police because in the middle of the summer, an autistic young man with poor blood circulation was wearing a ski mask and looked "sketchy." This was his only "crime."

"How do I not become the next young Black man killed by the police?" my brother continued. "The next one people write hashtags about and march for?"

I wanted to give him an answer, wanted to be able to tell him, "If you do *this*, it will never happen." Or, "Well the law says *this*, so officers aren't supposed to . . ." Or even, "You live in Toronto; don't worry about it." But I couldn't. I couldn't think of an answer to that question that wouldn't be a lie. And that's when Tyler said something that rocked me to my core.

"But Brian, you always have something. Some answer, some conversation to help guide me to an answer or tell me what to do for these types of things. You're a public defender who goes on TV every day to talk about crimes and police violence and trials. If you don't have the answer, then who does?" The tone in his voice wasn't filled with anger or disappointment. He was genuinely pleading with me, asking who would have these answers or who had more connections and knowledge of the criminal justice system than me. He wanted to know who could give him an answer because he *needed* this answer. And I had nothing for him. I did not have an answer to a simple question that every person has a right to ask: How do I stay safe?

So I turned back to the idea of writing a book, but the concept of bears in the woods and a park ranger wasn't enough to answer this question for my brother. Then I realized how the problem of not having an answer for my brother meant something else as well. *If I don't have this answer for my siblings, then it means I don't have it for my children.* After that, I put pen to paper in a way I hadn't before, thinking of how I wanted to write this book. This time, I had an idea for two stories about being falsely accused. The first one happened to me. I was stopped and questioned by the police on the New York City subway train—twice. Both times I was questioned because I "matched the description," which in NYC around 2009 was a "six-foot-four Black male with a short haircut." One of those times I was "escorted" off the train for further questioning. Both times I was released with a "warning" once the officers ran my name and concluded that I wasn't the person they were looking for.

The second story is one that I've seen in court dozens of times. A person who isn't an officer lies about being hit, threatened, or having their property—like a phone— taken. This situation can escalate to assault and police getting involved.

I wanted the stories I wrote to illustrate things that actually happen to preteens and teens, to include advice, and to depict conversations about staying safe when interacting with the police in public. Some of this information, like the importance of keeping your wallet in your front left pocket, I had. But I also talked to friends and colleagues and learned so much more.

I asked parents about the conversations they have with their children about police interactions. I asked parents of children of color, regardless of the parents' race. But I made sure every parent I talked to was connected to the criminal justice system. We discussed these situations both as parents and as victims of profiling, defense attorneys, former prosecutors, civil rights attorneys, judges, clerks, and peace officers. And after the many insightful conversations, I learned new lessons. Like how some people buy brightly colored wallets so officers don't confuse them for weapons. Or that you should "never argue from a position of weakness" and that it's important to avoid "giving others the power to make you react."

I used these conversations, insights, and lessons in different ways. Some I reflected on and allowed to guide me deeper into my stories. Some I wrote straight into the book. All of them got blended together into the stories of Reed and Olive.

As I wrote and interviewed, edited and rewrote, my wife became pregnant with our first child, a son. A son we decided to name in memory of my grandmother, Olive Reid.

Now, this story that began as a tool to help young people learn their rights and spark a conversation has become a story for my future son. And as it evolved into what it is, I started to realize what this book was and was not. It was not an indictment on the police. And it was not putting the responsibility on the victim, saying, "We must do X in order to be safe," and letting cops off the hook. This book is about taking the world as it is. It acknowledges that the number one concern of all good parents is keeping their children safe from harm. And that harm comes in many forms. When I, for example, taught my younger brother, "When the light says 'go,' look both ways before you walk through a crosswalk," I was taking the world as it is. Even though a car should stop for pedestrians because they have the right of way, I wanted to give my brother this lesson on staying safe.

My hope is that if a young adult, teenager, preteen, child, or person of any age anywhere asks an adult, "How do I not become another hashtag?" this book can help them find their answer. The only concern for me and this book is that our children come home safe. There is a time for conversations about reform, voting, protesting, solidarity, etc. I believe in all of those things, and so did the people I interviewed. But this book isn't the space for that. This book is about a different conversation. The constant theme among all the parents I spoke with, whatever their views of officers or the system, was that when speaking to their children about interacting with the police in public, the only point that mattered was the need to come home safe.

As I spoke with more people, I thought, *I can't keep this to myself. My siblings aren't the only ones asking me. My friends in the criminal justice system are struggling to find this answer. And if, after three years of law school, almost eight years of practicing, and four years of exclusive reporting on the criminal justice system, I didn't have the answer, then what about other parents?* I looked into sharing this book with the world.

I tried to tell the story in a way that says, "I don't have the answer," because even after all the interviewing and reflecting and research, I don't. No one person I spoke to had the answer. But my hope in sharing this book is that at least one piece of advice will help. Maybe we can all collectively learn from one another. If we can exchange our wisdom, be comforted that we are not alone in this search, and then spark a greater conversation, this book will have done its job.

Come Home Safe is for anyone who sees a person killed by the police for doing something that they do every day without thinking, like going for a jog, having a cell phone in their hand, or playing in a park. Because I know that it's probably not a matter of *if* my child asks me the same or similar question my brother asked but when. And for my son, my siblings, and any person who picks up this book, my answer is, "I'm sorry. I don't know. But this is what I learned."

Acknowledgments

Jeanessa Walker, Erica Birdsall Patterson, Ryan Patterson, Samantha Brewster Owens, Josh Laguerre, Ryan Wall, James Bell, Phillip Hamilton and Lance Clark from Hamilton and Clarke, LLP, Damien Brown, Jason Foy, Doug Rankin, Jamie Santana Jr., Peace Officer Al James, DeWitt Lacy, Ron Sylvestre, Aarmus Parker, Jeffery Storms, the Honorable Judge Craig Walker, Leslie Bernard Joseph, Marva Brown, Benton Reid, Emily Galvin-Almanza, Roslyn Morrison, Katherine Smith, Fabienne Pierre Goldgaber, Melba Pearson, Tammy Allison.

These are the mothers and fathers I interviewed to put this book together. The people who have honored me by sharing their stories and wisdom. I hope this work reflects their brilliance.